Haunted Tales

A MARY O'REILLY PARANORMAL MYSTERY

(Book Fifteen)

by

Terri Reid

HAUNTED TALES – A MARY O'REILLY
PARANORMAL MYSTERY

by

Terri Reid

The author would like to thank all those who have contributed to the creation of this book: Richard Reid, Sarah Powers, Denise Carpenter, Maureen Marella, Jennifer Bates and Hillary Gadd. I especially wanted to express my love and gratitude to my "clever mommy" Virginia Onines who has always supported my dreams and has offered loving advice.

She would also like to thank all of the wonderful readers who walk with her through Mary and Bradley's adventures and encourage her along the way. I hope we continue on this wonderful journey for a long time.

Prologue

Kristen Banks adjusted the transistor radio on her desk to pick up the station that seemed to be fading out; she turned the knob to the left slowly and then reversed the movement, turning it to the right until the station once again came in clearly. It was hard to pick up the popular AM Chicago radio station all the way in Polo, especially within the confines of the school, but the solid rock music was worth the effort.

Singing along to "Could It Be I'm Falling in Love," she pulled another piece of narrow, lined paper off the stack of spelling tests and quickly reviewed it. With a frustrated sigh, she picked up the red pencil and marked the first three words. "Really, Andrew?" she muttered softly. "Did you even study the words at all?"

Even though Andrew was only a fourth grader, Kristen could see that he had potential, but if he didn't buckle down and start studying, he was going to fall short of the person he could be. She counted the number of red checks on the paper; he only got six of the twenty-four words correct. With a heavy heart she placed a red "F" on the top of the page but next to it wrote, "You have the ability to do much better than this. I believe in you. You should believe in yourself."

The radio's jingle interrupted her paper grading, and she glanced up at the clock above the bulletin boards. It was already past seven. Where did the time go?

She sat back in her chair, picked up the latest letter from her fiancé that was lying on the top of her inbox and smiled. "This is where all the time went," she murmured, a soft smile playing across her lips. "I'm daydreaming about you again, Danny."

Pulling the thin sheet from the airmail envelope, she reread the closing lines once again, although they were already burned into her memory.

My deployment ends in two weeks. I'm doing everything I can to stay safe because all I want is to hold you in my arms again. I can't wait until we stand before our families and friends and I can hear you say the words, "I do." So, I've been thinking we should get married right away. As soon as I get home. Between my mom and your mom, I know we can pull this off. I love you with all my heart.

Yours forever,
Danny

Yes, she could pull it off! She leaned back in her chair and smiled up at the ceiling. She would *love* to pull it off! And, as soon as she got home that evening, she was going to give both moms a call so their quick wedding would be perfect. She looked down at the open journal that was next to the ink blotter on her desk and jotted down a few more items under her newly created list, *Things for my wedding.* She used to keep her journal at home but found that she had more time to write her thoughts during the week when she was sitting at her desk.

She turned to the next page and wrote, *Give Andrew's mom a call about study habits for Andrew.* She often used her journal to write down thoughts and reminders about her students and their parents, thoughts that might not be appropriate for her teacher's notes.

A noise in the hallway interrupted her thoughts, and she looked at the glass pane on the classroom window. She could see a shadow moving down the hall, but the lights were too dim for her to get a clear view. She knew it wasn't the janitor; he'd already gone home for the day. A shiver of apprehension went down her back as she realized that everyone who worked at the school had probably gone home for the day.

She shook her head. "So what?" she chided herself. This was Polo, Illinois. This was her home town. People kept their doors unlocked and the keys in their cars. There was nothing to be afraid of in Polo. Perhaps it was just a concerned parent coming to meet with her.

She opened the desk drawer to her right and lifted up the secret compartment under the floor of the drawer where she kept her journal and her letters from Danny. She loved having them near, too, but didn't want someone to accidentally come across them or her journal. So, sixteen months ago, when she received his first letter, she added a false compartment that was only a few inches high and fairly undetectable. She put the letter into the journal and slipped them both into the compartment. For some reason, she felt the letter and her journal were safer in the compartment until she dealt with her unexpected visitor.

Pushing her chair back, she walked across the room to the door and opened it. "Hello?" she called out into the hallway. "Can I help you?"

She looked up and down the hall. No one was there. "That's odd," she murmured.

The hairs on the back of her neck stood up, and she stepped back into her classroom, turning the lock into the closed position. She wrapped her arms across her body and took a deep, calming breath. "You're being ridiculous," she said to herself. "It was just a reflection of a passing car."

She looked around her classroom, the desks neatly lined up in six rows, the bulletin boards filled with recent art projects. The counter held their science projects, sprouting bean seeds in paper cups lined up under the window, and a map was pulled down to highlight Illinois for Social Studies the next day. She tried to let these familiar sights instill a feeling of normality. But the lump in her stomach just seemed to grow larger as her heart pounded in her chest.

"Okay, I'm just scaring myself now," she admitted. "I might as well work from home because I'm going to be jumping at every little sound I hear."

Walking to her desk, she gathered the unmarked papers together and placed them in her leather briefcase, along with her favorite marking pens, a red one and a black one, and her smiley-face stickers. She closed up her desk, pulled her jacket and purse from the small teacher's closet behind her desk and unlocked her door.

She hated that she peered up and down the hall before she stepped out of the classroom, but there was no one there to witness it so what did it matter. The hallway was empty. She stepped out, put the key into the lock and locked the door before sticking the key securely into the outside pocket of her purse.

Taking a deep breath, she shook her head. "All safe and sound," she said.

"Not quite," a low voice from behind her whispered.

Her scream was swallowed as a large hand was clapped over her mouth. She struggled against the strong arm that pulled her back against a hard body and held her tightly. "I just want you to be mine," the low voice whispered in her ear. "I know

5

you think you love someone else, but that's just because you ain't really had a chance to get to know me."

She tried to shake her head and pull away. She tried to scream. But the large hand was also covering her nose, and she was finding it hard to breathe. She felt herself moving, being pulled backwards toward the staircase.

"You'll be happier with me," the voice continued, and she trembled with repulsion as she felt wet lips graze alongside her neck. "I'll give you the kind of loving a woman like you needs."

Her vision was dimming, and she knew that in a matter of moments she would lose consciousness and be totally vulnerable. The hand moved lower, stroking up and down her hip.

"Your body was just made for me," the voice said, and the grip tightened once more and pulled her forcefully back. "And I'm gonna show you a real good time."

With fury born of desperation, she lifted her leg and kicked back, her high heel connecting with something solid.

"You bitch!" the voice roared. The hands whipped her around and pushed her back.

She didn't have a chance to focus on a face. A scream exploded from her mouth as she stumbled backwards onto the open staircase and fell. She bounced against the concrete and steel stairs, felt the pain rip through her bones, and finally as her head collided with the wrought iron railings, she felt nothing at all.

Chapter One

"So, there I was as this thing came hurtling down the staircase towards me," Bradley said, waving his arms over his head for drama. "And Mary was unconscious on the couch from a terrible head-on collision she had with a fort."

"A fort?" Mike asked, leaning against the kitchen wall with his arms folded over his chest, engrossed in the story.

"A fort?" Clarissa echoed, turning her focus from her father to her mother as they all sat around the breakfast table.

Mary chuckled. "That's another story," she replied. "And I wasn't unconscious. I was just sleeping."

"Sleeping, unconscious, what's the difference?" Bradley asked with a wink.

"Well, as a former first responder, I can tell you…" Mike interrupted.

"So, this terrible creature…" Bradley continued, talking over Mike.

"That you couldn't see," Mary inserted with a wink towards Mike.

"Which made it even more terrible," Bradley added. "Came down the stairs. Thump. Thump. Thump."

"Like the bunny in Bambi?" Clarissa asked innocently, sending both Mary and Mike a conspiratorial smile.

"No, not like that at all," Bradley replied, so caught up in the story that he didn't see the smile pass among his audience. "It was more like this."

He lifted his boot-clad foot and thumped it against the kitchen linoleum. Thump. Thump. Thump.

"Very realistic," Mike said. "I can totally picture it."

"Oh," Clarissa replied, hiding a grin. "I get it now."

He looked up and studied their faces. "Do you want a ghost story or not?" he growled, the twinkle in his eyes belying the tone of his voice.

"Of course I do, Daddy," Clarissa replied. "'Sides, you have to practice telling it for Halloween night when everyone's here."

He nodded and continued. "So, I drew my gun…"

"You were going to shoot a ghost?" Clarissa asked.

9

"Well, I didn't believe in ghosts at the time," he replied.

"You were going to shoot an invisible Thumper?" Clarissa asked while Mary stifled a chuckle.

"Wow, that's like shooting an invisible Bambi's mother," Mike added.

"I was merely being prepared for anything," he replied. "So then I stealthily made my way across the room."

Remembering the remains of her treasured cookie jar that he broke during that encounter, Mary gently cleared her throat, and he smiled up at her.

"Perhaps not as stealthily as I would have liked," he admitted. "But I stood between the creature and Mary."

"Yes he did," Mary agreed. "He protected me from Earl."

"Earl?" Clarissa and Mike asked.

"Yes, and Earl was a ghastly looking specter," Mary added, lowering her voice. "With a body riddled with bullet holes and blood oozing from each wound."

"Ohhhhh," Clarissa said, her eyes widening.

"And he walked with a slow limp," Mary continued, "dragging his bloodied body through the house and up the stairs to my bedroom where I lay sleeping, alone and unprotected."

Clarissa grabbed hold of her father's hand. "Oh, no," she said.

Mike leaned forward in spite of himself.

"And when I looked up to see him standing next to my bed, blood dripping on my white blanket…" Mary said.

"Did it stain?" Clarissa interrupted, lifting her hand from Bradley's and turning to Mary.

Bradley looked from daughter to mother and laughed. "Whose daughter is she?"

Mary chuckled and shook her head. "No, surprisingly, it didn't," she said. "But I was worried."

"Wait," Mike said. "A headless, dead guy was in your bedroom, and you were worried about his blood staining your duvet?"

"It was a really nice duvet," Mary replied.

"And then she looked up from her bed," Bradley continued, his voice mimicking Mary's. "And what did she discover? He was holding his head in his hands."

"Cause he had a headache?" Clarissa asked.

11

Mike exploded in laughter and then clapped his hand over his mouth. "Sorry," he said to Bradley.

Bradley exhaled in frustration. "No, because someone chopped his head off," he said, and then he turned to Mary. "I am absolutely no good at this. Your entire family is going to fall asleep during my story."

Clarissa turned back to her father. "Oh, no, Daddy," she encouraged. "You were really great. You really made me feel scared. Really."

He bent over and placed a kiss on the top of her head. "Well, thank you, sweetheart," he replied with a smile. "That makes me feel a lot better."

"So, when are Grandma and Grandpa O'Reilly and my uncles coming to tell ghost stories?" Clarissa asked.

"Halloween night," Mary said. "So we'll go trick or treating early, and then we'll all get together, light the jack-o-lantern and tell scary stories." She paused for a moment, looked over her daughter's head to Bradley and winked. "I know. You could tell them about the time you helped Clarissa clean out under her bed. That was really scary."

Clarissa giggled.

"Scary and disgusting," Bradley added, and then he glanced up at the clock. "Okay, kiddo, the

12

bus will be here in five minutes. Go brush your teeth and grab your backpack."

"Okay," she replied with a smile. "I can't wait until Halloween."

"Me, too," Bradley said, his voice a little less enthusiastic. "I just can't wait."

"Don't worry," Mike teased as he started to fade away. "You'll get better. You can't possible get any worse."

Chapter Two

"So she doesn't suspect a thing?" Rosie asked Bradley, placing a blueberry muffin on a plate before him.

"Course she don't," Stanley answered before Bradley could speak. "He's a law enforcement officer. He knows how to keep a secret."

Stanley picked up another muffin from the middle of their kitchen table and slowly peeled the paper from its sides. "However..." he started.

"However?" Bradley asked, his mouth half full.

Stanley turned and met Bradley's eyes. "However, iffen you keep eating my wife's cooking after you eat your wife's cooking every morning, she's gonna wonder which of the two of you this baby shower is for."

Bradley paused, the second bite of muffin halfway to his mouth, and looked down at his waistline. "I work out," he said defensively.

"Besides," Rosie added, defending him. "It's very normal for men to gain weight while their wives are pregnant."

Bradley put the muffin back on his plate. "I'm not gaining weight," he said. "Am I?"

"No, of course not," Rosie said, patting his arm. "You look just fine."

"Fer a middle-aged man," Stanley added.

Bradley pushed back his chair, stood up, gave Rosie a hug and nodded to Stanley. "I'd better be getting in to the office," he said. "If you need me to get anything for the shower or do anything, don't hesitate to ask."

"Thank you, Bradley," she replied. "But between Margaret and Kate, I think we have it all covered."

"Excellent," he replied. "Thanks again. She is going to be so surprised."

He left the house and walked over to the cruiser, but before getting in, he stared at his reflection in the mirror. *Am I getting a little thick around the middle?* he asked himself as he turned first one way and then the other.

Stanley chuckled loudly from behind the curtain on the front window as he watched Bradley.

"Stanley, that was mean," Rosie said, holding back her own chuckle. "You know as well as I do that Bradley hasn't put on an ounce of weight since he's been married."

15

"A man's gotta do what he's gotta do to protect his wife's blueberry muffins," Stanley replied. "'Sides, a little work out in the gym will help him release some of that anxiety that's eating him."

"He only has anxiety because you keep teasing him," she replied.

"Toughen the boy up," Stanley said with a grin. "Good for him."

Shaking her head, Rosie walked back into the kitchen. "You know, Stanley," she said. "I've been thinking about what you said. And I think that perhaps we ought to start eating better. You know, more salads and fruit. Fewer baked goods."

"What?" Stanley asked, dropping the curtain and hurrying back to the kitchen. "What are you talking about woman?"

She turned from the sink and grinned at him. "Gotcha!"

"You nearly scared the life out of me," he said with a smile, walking across the room and enfolding her in his arms. "I sure didn't marry you because you were a good cook, but I ain't complaining about it."

She laid her head on his shoulder. "Oh, Stanley," she said. "I'm the luckiest woman in the world."

He smiled down at her. "Well, that makes perfect sense," he said softly. "Seeing as I'm the luckiest man."

"Well, luckiest man," she said, stepping back. "How are we going to get Mary to her own baby shower without letting her know anything is wrong?"

"You just leave that to me," he said.

"You've got a plan?" she asked hopefully.

"Well, no," he admitted with a wink. "But don't you worry; I got a whole week to figure this out."

Chapter Three

Clarissa hurried down the bus aisle and slipped into the seat next to her best friend, Maggie Brennan. She sat quietly until everyone else at their bus stop had taken their seats and the bus driver had closed the door and started moving down the street. Then she turned to her friend and quietly whispered, "I need you to help me with a surprise."

Maggie smiled and nodded. "I love surprises," she said. "What kind of surprise?"

"On Halloween we're having a ghost story telling party," Clarissa said.

"I know," Maggie replied, her eyes sparkling with delight. "My family gets to come, too."

"Oh, cool!" Clarissa replied. "Then you know."

"Know what?"

"That everyone is supposed to tell a ghost story," Clarissa said.

Maggie shook her head. "No," she said, her eyes widening in interest. "I didn't know that at all."

Clarissa nodded eagerly. "Yes. Everyone is supposed to tell one," she explained.

"Do they have to be spooky?"

Shrugging, Clarissa thought about the question for a moment. "I don't know. But I don't think so. Not all of Mary's stories are spooky ones."

"Whew," Maggie said, leaning back in the seat. "That's a relief. I have lots of ghost stories, but none of them are spooky."

"But that's the thing," Clarissa said.

"What?" Maggie asked.

"You have lots of ghost stories. Mary has *lots* of ghost stories, and even my dad has ghost stories," she explained. "But I don't have any ghost stories. At all."

"Oh," Maggie replied. "And you want to have one, right?"

Clarissa nodded again. "Right," she said. "I need a ghost story."

"Okay," Maggie said with a smile. "I'll tell you one of my stories, and then you can pretend that it's yours."

Shaking her head, Clarissa faced her friend. "No, that won't work," she explained. "It has to be my story, or it won't be as good."

"But you can't see ghosts," Maggie reasoned.

19

"Remember when you taught me how to jump double-dutch?" Clarissa asked.

Maggie nodded.

"Well, you taught me how to do that," Clarissa reasoned. "So, you can teach me how to see ghosts."

Maggie thought about it for a moment. "I don't think it's that easy."

"Well, double-dutch wasn't easy at all, and you still taught me."

"But I don't know how I learned," Maggie said. "I just did it one day."

Clarissa folded her arms over her chest and sat back in her seat, thinking about what Maggie had just said. The bus rumbled farther down the route and pulled to the side of the road to pick up another group of children. Waiting until the bus was moving again, Clarissa turned back to Maggie. "Well, maybe if you could try to remember what happened the first time you saw a ghost," she said slowly, thinking it through as she voiced it, "maybe you could tell me, and then I could do it."

"I was pretty little," Maggie said, her nose wrinkled in concern. "I don't know if I can remember all the way back then."

"Please?" Clarissa implored.

"Okay," Maggie said, biting her lower lip in concentration. "The one thing I remember is that I first started seeing ghosts when I looked sideways."

"You looked sideways?" Clarissa asked. "What does that mean?"

Sitting back her in her seat, Maggie kept her face frozen forward while she moved her eyes to look at Clarissa sitting beside her. "Like this," she said.

"What?" Clarissa asked.

Maggie huffed with frustration. "Look at my eyes," she said, keeping her face forward.

Clarissa leaned forward and looked at Maggie's face. "Oh, only your eyes are looking sideways," she said. "I get it."

Maggie blinked and then turned her head. "Yeah, I remember that I saw more ghosts when I looked sideways at them," she said. "And sometimes they would disappear when I turned and looked at them."

"Were they shy?"

Maggie shrugged. "Maybe," she said. "But that's all I remember."

Clarissa sat back in her seat facing forward and slid her eyes to the side. "I don't see anything," she whispered to Maggie.

"That's 'cause there aren't any ghosts on the bus," Maggie said. "It only works when there are actually ghosts around you."

"Oh, yeah," Clarissa giggled. "I forgot."

Chapter Four

Mary shivered in her chair and glanced up to see if her office door was open. She was surprised to see a middle-aged man sheepishly walk from the door towards her desk.

"I'm sorry," he stammered nervously. "I'm probably in the wrong place."

Mary smiled up at him and slowly rose from her chair, pushing against the armrests to leverage her decidedly pregnant body into a standing position.

"You're pregnant," he blurted out.

Her smile widened. "Yes, I know," she said with gentle humor.

Shaking his head nervously, he exhaled softly. "Of course you know," he said with chagrin. "I'm such an idiot. I really should be leaving."

"Wait," she exclaimed, holding out her hand as she slowly walked across the room. "Don't make me waste all of that effort."

His eyes widened in horror, and then he saw the smile on her face and relaxed. "Sorry," he said again with a sheepish smile. "I've never done anything like this before."

Biting back a chuckle, Mary leaned back against her desk. "Like what?" she asked.

He looked around her office. "You know, been to a psychic or anything like that."

"Well, I hate to disappoint you," she replied. "But you still haven't been to a psychic. I'm a private investigator."

"But I thought..." he stammered. "I came here..."

He looked around helplessly.

"I can see and communicate with ghosts," she said. "But I don't look into the future or read palms or find missing items. I just have the ability to communicate with some dead people."

"How? How can you do that?" he asked.

"Well, it all happened the night that I died," she replied.

He stared at her, his jaw dropping, and stepped backwards to the door. "You think you're dead?" he asked.

She shook her head. "I got better," she said, trying to keep a straight face. She looked at the fear in his eyes and took pity on him. It really wasn't his fault that he was slightly awkward. "I died on the operating table and had an out-of-body experience. I even went towards the light." She paused for a

24

moment and met his eyes. "I was given a choice. I could continue on or go back and live. I could be with my family. I could live my life. But things would be different for me."

She folded her arms loosely over her belly and sighed. "So, I came back," she said. "And found, to my great surprise, that now I could see and communicate with ghosts who were stuck here, on this side of the light, because they needed someone alive to help them move on."

His face lost the look of fear and he stepped toward her. "So, you're for real?"

She shrugged and nodded. "Pretty much," she said. "I'm in the profession of helping people move on, and sometimes that means I'm solving crimes. But sometimes it means I just have to do research. Pretty average private investigative work."

He studied her for a moment. "How much do you charge?" he asked.

"Well, when you have ghosts for clients, you really can't expect to make too much money," she replied. "Generally, I end up working for free. But the disability income from the Chicago Police Department makes up the difference."

"You can't work because you were shot?" he asked.

Mary sighed. *This isn't going to help at all,* she thought. "No," she said honestly. "I can't work because I see ghosts. That either classifies me for disability because I'm psychologically unstable, or, as my friend and psychiatrist Gracie puts it, I got too much going on to concentrate on my job."

He actually smiled, and Mary felt herself relax. "You don't seem crazy," he ventured.

"Why, thank you," she replied.

Once again, he flushed with embarrassment and started to step back. "I'm so sorry," he faltered. "I can't believe I said that."

Mary laughed and shook her head. "Don't worry about it," she said. "Now tell me why you decided to come here today."

He reached into his back pocket and pulled out a narrow piece of laminated paper that was folded in fourths. He unfolded the paper and handed it to her. She looked down at a spelling test that was obviously done by a child. Most of the words had been spelled incorrectly, and there was a bright red 'F" at the top of the page with red writing that was nearly faded. Mary squinted at the words, trying to read them.

He gently took the paper back from her. "I'll read it to you. *You have the ability to do much better than this. I believe in you. You should believe in yourself,*" he said, and then he looked up and met her eyes. "My name is Andrew Tyler, and I need you to help me find who murdered my fourth grade teacher."

Chapter Five

Mary picked up her bottle of water, took a sip and then sat down in her chair on the other side of the desk from Andrew. She picked up a yellow note pad and pen. "Okay, why don't you give me the details, and I'll see if this is a case I can help you with," she said.

He nodded. "Okay," he replied. "Her name was Miss Banks, Kristen Banks, and she was a fourth grade teacher at Centennial Grammar School in Polo in the mid-seventies. It was a couple weeks before Spring Break, and she was engaged to a soldier who was serving in Vietnam."

He paused and took a deep breath.

"She must have been working late, after school," he said, nervously brushing his hair off his forehead. "The janitor found her in the morning. They said she'd tripped down the stairs and struck her head on the rail. They said it was an accident, a horrible accident."

Mary looked up from her notes. "But you don't think it was an accident?" she asked.

Shaking his head, he nervously tapped his fingers together. After a moment, he took a deep breath and leaned closer to the desk. "I saw her," he said, lowering his voice. "After she was dead. I saw her."

Mary leaned back in her chair. "What did you see?"

Shrugging, trying to remain casual although Mary could see the emotion he was trying to contain, he continued, "They kept us in the same classroom but brought in a substitute to teach us for the rest of the year. Often, I'd glance up, and I'd see her, for just a moment, standing next to her desk. And the look on her face…"

He stopped and took a deep breath. "She looked so sad," he said. "So incredibly sad. She would look out at all of us and slowly shake her head. Then she would look directly at me, and she would say something. But I couldn't hear it. I couldn't understand it."

Clasping his hands together tightly, he stared down at them intently. Finally, he looked back up, his eyes glistening with unshed tears. "They told me that the last thing she did before she died was grade my spelling test," he said, his voice thick with emotion. "The last thing she did was take the time to write me a note that she believed in me and that I needed to believe in myself. That note changed my life."

"Perhaps she was sad because she couldn't be with you and the rest of the students," Mary suggested. "Perhaps it was her regret that she couldn't continue making a difference."

"No," he said decisively, shaking his head. "No, it just doesn't make sense. She was really athletic. She would dash up and down those stairs a couple of times a day. And now, as an adult, as I review the accident and the momentum it would have taken for her to not only fall but also crack her skull on the railings, I believe she was pushed."

"Didn't the police look into it?" she asked.

He shook his head. "No, they just decided it was an accident," he said. "I've always thought it was more than an accident, so much so that I bought the old school when it was put up for sale."

"You bought it?" she asked incredulously.

"Yeah, they were going to tear it down," he said. "And I knew that any evidence would be gone when the school was gone, so I bought it. But, the city still wants to condemn it. They've only given me a couple of months."

Mary put down the pad and the pencil. "Okay, this is really impressive, and you've done a great deal for your former teacher," she said. "But I don't know if walking through an empty school building is going to produce anything."

"It's not empty," he replied.

"What?" she asked.

"When the new school was built about twenty years ago, they didn't want any of the old furnishings. They wanted everything to be new, so I added a contingency to the purchase that I got to keep all of the furnishings," he said, "desks, tables, chairs and even some of the older library books. Anything they didn't use in the new school, I bought."

"Have you been back to your old classroom?" she asked.

He nodded. "Yeah," he said. "I've been doing a little investigating on my own."

Mary studied him for a long moment. "This means a lot to you, doesn't it?" she asked.

"Yes," he said emphatically. "She changed my life. I owe her so much. I feel like I can't rest until I find out, once and for all, if her death was just an accident or if she was murdered."

"Well, I guess we should take a look," she said.

His face broke into a wide smile. "Thank you," he said, standing up and leaning over the desk to shake her hand. "Thank you so much."

Mary shook her head. "I haven't done anything yet," she said.

31

"That's okay," he replied. "I know you will. I believe in you."

Chapter Six

"There are ghosts in the library?" Clarissa whispered, following Maggie into the children's section of the library, in the far southeast corner.

"Shhhhh," Maggie said, looking over her shoulder to make sure her mother wasn't close by. Kate Brennan, Maggie's mother, had picked the girls up after school and brought them to the library. "I told my mom that we had to come here to work on our special Halloween school project. She doesn't know we're also looking for ghosts."

"But ghosts are here, right?" Clarissa insisted.

"Sometimes," Maggie said. "Ghosts like to hang around old stuff, like old books, so sometimes they're here."

"Okay, I'm going to start looking for them, too," Clarissa said, moving her eyes to one side as she walked alongside the book stacks.

"Just be careful," Maggie cautioned.

"What? Ouch!" Clarissa cried as she walked into a tall bookshelf.

The Youth Services librarian hurried across the room from her desk. "Are you okay?" she asked, bending over to examine the red mark on Clarissa's forehead.

Tears shining in her eyes, Clarissa nodded. "Uh huh," she replied, embarrassed and achy. "I'm fine."

"Did you trip?" the woman asked, looking around for a ripple in the carpet or some other obstruction that would have caused the accident.

Clarissa shook her head. "No," she admitted. "I just didn't see it."

"But you were walking towards it," the librarian said, confused.

Clarissa sighed. How was she going to explain that she was looking sideways instead of forward? Looking for ghosts was hard. Then she had a thought, and her face brightened. "My mom once walked into a fort that she didn't see," she supplied. "I guess it runs in the family."

The librarian looked even more confused. "Well, I suppose so," she said, standing up, "As long as you're okay."

"I'm fine," Clarissa said, pasting a smile on her face. "Really."

As soon as the librarian turned around, Maggie grabbed Clarissa's hand and pulled her down the aisle between the stacks to a small table tucked into a hidden corner. She helped Clarissa into a chair and hugged her. "Are you okay?" she asked.

A few tears slipped down Clarissa's cheek, but she nodded at her friend. "I'm fine," she sniffed. "But I don't think I'm going to look for ghosts in the library anymore."

"Don't worry, Clarissa," Maggie said. "I can find a ghost for you. This is one of my special ghost places."

Clarissa wiped her eyes and looked around slowly. "There's a ghost here?" she whispered.

Maggie nodded and pointed to a darkened corner with some leather-bound books behind a glass case. Clarissa's eyes widened in amazement as the glass case opened by itself and a book slowly slid from its place and floated in the air. Then it settled on its back and opened wide, the pages slowly flipping from front to back.

"The books are floating," she whispered excitedly. "They are actually floating."

Maggie shook her head. "No, there's a ghost in the aisle taking the book out and looking through it," she said.

"There's a ghost in there? Really?" Clarissa exclaimed. "I want to see it."

"Try squinting your eyes," Maggie said.

Clarissa scrunched up her face and squinted as hard as she could.

"Can you see him?" Maggie asked.

Clarissa shook her head. "No, and the squinting makes my head hurt."

"Try looking sideways," Maggie suggested.

Clarissa moved her head so it was facing forward and then she moved her eyes sideways. The air in front of the glass case seemed to ripple, like the air above a sidewalk in the summertime. "I think something's happening," she said excitedly. "The air is wiggling."

Maggie nodded. "Keep it up," she said. "I think it's working."

Clarissa tried to bring the wiggles into focus, but they just remained soft and blurry. "I don't see anything but blurs."

Maggie sighed. "Well, at least you saw something. Maybe it's going to take some practice."

Staring at the wiggling air for a few more moments, Clarissa nodded. "Yeah," she agreed. "It took me a really long time to learn Double Dutch."

"And the books floating in the air is pretty scary," Maggie said. "Maybe you could tell that story."

"The books were cool," Clarissa agreed, turning her eyes to look at her friend. "But I want something even better."

"I'll see if my mom can bring us back here tomorrow after school," Maggie said. "Then we can practice again."

"Thanks, Maggie," Clarissa said. "You're my best friend ever."

Chapter Seven

Bradley was standing in front of the hall mirror when Mary entered the house that afternoon.

"Do I look like I'm gaining weight?" he asked, standing sideways and critically assessing himself.

Mary looked down at her protruding belly and then back at the slim, muscular man she loved. "Are you kidding me?" she asked, dropping her briefcase on the table next to the door. "Do you really want to go there?"

He glanced over his shoulder at his wife and shook his head. "But you're not fat," he said. "You're pregnant and, actually, pretty damn sexy, too." He looked back in the mirror. "But Stanley said he thought I was getting a little thick around the middle."

Holding back a smile, Mary walked up behind him. She slid her arms around his waist, as far as her arms would reach with her belly in the way, and said, "Were you, by chance, eating any of Rosie's cooking that Stanley would prefer not sharing?" she asked.

He looked at her reflection, and his eyes widened. "Well, yeah, I was eating a blueberry muffin," he replied.

"And did you take a second muffin once he made the comment?" she asked.

"No," he said. "No, I didn't."

Mary grinned at him. "He's playing with your mind, Chief," she said with a wink.

A sigh of relief passed through Bradley's lips. "I didn't think I was gaining weight," he said shaking his head. "He had me glancing at my reflection all day."

"Well, from my perspective," Mary said, "that would have been a lovely way to spend the day."

He slowly turned around and wrapped his arms around her, lowering his face to kiss her thoroughly. "Did I happen to mention how sexy you look when you're pregnant?" he asked, kissing her jawline.

She moaned softly. "Did I happen to mention that Clarissa was going with the Brennans to the library after school today and is going to be coming home a little late?" she sighed.

Bradley lifted his head and looked down at his wife with a smile. "I've been reading about exercising during pregnancy," he murmured, slowly running his hands across her back and pulling her even closer.

"You have?" she whispered back.

He lowered his head to her neck and nibbled against the sensitive skin on her collarbone. Her skin began to warm, and her heart pounded in her chest. "Um, hmmm," he said. "It's supposed to be very, very good for you."

He reached up and unbuttoned the top button of her blouse and continued his exploration against her soft skin. "Good for me?" she stuttered, feeling her knees going weak and leaning against him.

He looked up, met her eyes, and her heart skipped a beat. The passion and hunger she saw in his eyes were genuine, and her body responded in kind. "Mary, we need to go upstairs," he whispered hoarsely. "Now."

A shiver coursed through her body, and she exhaled softly. Then she shrieked when he bent over and scooped her up in his arms. "Bradley, put me down," she insisted. "You're going to hurt yourself."

He kissed her again, taking his time to explore the nuances of her lips, taste her passion and demonstrate his own desire. Finally, breathing heavily, he lifted his head and looked down at her.

Panting, she wrapped her arms around his neck. "Bradley," she pleaded softly. "Carry me upstairs. I don't think I can walk anymore."

A satisfied smile curled his lips, and he lifted her even further in his arms. "It will be my pleasure," he replied, his voice laced with desire. "And yours too, I hope."

She laid her head against his chest, feeling the strength of his flexed muscle and hearing the steadiness of his heartbeat. "I'm sure it will be," she murmured, reaching up to kiss his neck. "I'm sure it will be."

Chapter Eight

"Are you sure you don't want me to come with you?" Bradley asked later that evening as Mary prepared to meet Andrew in Polo.

"Where are you going, Mom?" Clarissa asked from the kitchen table where she was working on a school project.

"I'm going to walk through an old school," she replied, slipping an oversized, black sweatshirt over her head and then over her belly. "A man wants me to help him find his fourth grade teacher."

She turned to Bradley and smiled. "I'm fine," she said. "Besides, you have to practice your ghost-telling skills on Clarissa."

"Yeah, I need to hear more about Earl," Clarissa added. "It was getting scary. Really."

Bradley shook his head and lowered his voice. "It's slightly humiliating when your eight-year-old daughter is trying to boost your confidence," he said.

She smiled wickedly at him and ran her hand slowly up his arm. "Well, from where I'm standing you don't need any boost in your confidence," she whispered.

He smiled back down at her and nodded. "Same goes," he whispered back. "You still take my breath away."

"Yeah, well, that was from carrying me upstairs," she teased.

He laughed and placed a quick kiss on her lips. "Be careful and hurry home," he said.

"I promise," she replied and then turned to Clarissa. "I'm driving past the store on my way down to Polo. Do you need anything?"

"Did you get candy for the Halloween party at school?" she asked.

"Thanks for reminding me," Mary replied. "I'll stop by and get some. Anything special?"

"No peanuts," Clarissa said. "That's the rules."

"Got it," Mary said. "No peanuts."

"But, if a bag of candy bars with peanuts and caramel happens to make it into the cart," Bradley whispered, "I'll take care of them."

She grinned. "Oh, I see we aren't worried about gaining weight anymore."

"Not if I'm exercising regularly," he countered with a wink. "Besides, I'll share."

"Well then, you've got a deal," she replied. Then she raised her voice back to its normal level. "Okay you two, have fun telling ghost stories. I'll be back in a couple of hours."

"Have fun," Clarissa called.

"Thanks," she replied as she picked up her purse and headed for the door.

The autumn evening was crisp and clear. The moon was just above the horizon and was nearly full. Mary hoped it would be full for Halloween night. There was nothing like a full moon for trick-or-treating.

She drove south on Highway 26 past the last retail area in town and onto the rural farmland that surrounded the city. A few large combines were in the fields harvesting the last of the corn crop, their headlights glaring brightly as they moved up and down the rows. Mary kept her eyes on the road, trying to avoid the blinding light.

She moved away from the combines and reduced her speed a little as she entered one of the smaller towns. Fields gave way to houses that lined the highway, their lawns neatly manicured and covered with gold and red leaves from the maple and oak trees standing lookout in the front yards. Windows glowed with warm light that was soft and inviting, but the porches were a fearsome collection of the decorations of the season: pumpkins, inflatable ghosts, cardboard coffins and other spooky creatures that Mary knew delighted the children in the community as they looked forward to Halloween night.

She continued down the highway, and twenty minutes later she was pulling up in the large parking lot in front of the school. The asphalt of the parking lot was fractured, and weeds had sprung up between the cracks, creating a squiggly patchwork of crumbled blacktop, solid surface and dried plants. Carefully driving across the lot, she pulled up as close to the front door as she could.

Stepping out of the car, she took a long look at the old school. The two-story tall portico was supported by ornate columns that in early days, Mary thought, must have been beautiful. But now the ceiling of the decorative entranceway was rotted and splintered. The paint on the columns was nearly non-existent, and what remained was yellowed and chipped. Mary stepped carefully over the broken boards and rubbish that lay in front of the entranceway and walked to the front door. Peering through the broken front window, Mary tried to see into the interior of the school, but it was too dark inside to see anything.

"Excuse me, can I help you?" said a male voice.

Mary turned to see an older man walking towards her from the backyard across the alley from the school, wiping his hands on a rag. Mary glanced behind him and saw the automobile he'd evidently been working on. "Hi," she said. "Sorry to interrupt you. I'm here to meet someone."

"You don't look like a demolition expert," he replied with a shake of his head. "That's all this old school needs, a date with a wrecking ball."

She sighed. He was probably right. "That's so sad," she said. "It looks like it once was a great building."

He nodded. "Yes, my wife, her brothers and even her father attended that school," he said. "They have good memories of it. But now, it's an eyesore and a danger."

"Danger?" Mary asked.

He put his hands on his hips and shook his head. "One of these days a good wind is just going to blow it over," he said, and then he winked at her. "Just teasing you, girl."

He paused for a moment and studied her. "Hey, don't I know you?" he asked.

Mary shrugged. "I've never really been in Polo before tonight," she confessed.

He snapped his fingers decisively. "That's it, you're that gal from the paper," he said. "Think you can see ghosts."

Mary closed her eyes for a moment and sighed. Would she ever stop regretting her decision to do that article?

"Yes, that was me," she admitted. "I'm Mary O'Reilly."

"Dale. Dale Epperly. I had an aunt who saw ghosts," he said, nodding his head. "Course, she also talked with the barnyard animals, so we never did pay her no mind."

"Well, thank you for that," Mary replied, not quite sure how she should respond.

Dale nodded. "Sure, no problem," he said earnestly, and then he motioned with his head in the direction of the car. "Well, since you ain't no arsonist, guess I'll get back to my car."

"Yes, please," Mary insisted. "Don't let me stop you."

He nodded his head at her and then walked back across the alley to peer underneath the hood of his car. A moment later she heard the rattle of the door in front of her and looked up as Andrew pushed the school's door open. "Sorry to keep you waiting," he said, stepping out into the night air. "Thanks so much for meeting me here."

Mary pointedly looked around and then turned back to Andrew. "Are you sure it's safe to go in there?" she asked.

He nodded. "Oh sure," he said. "This place was built like a rock." Lifting a hand, he slapped it against one of the pillars, and Mary had to jump out of the way when a shower of rotted wood rained down on them.

"What kind of rock?" she asked skeptically.

He shook his head and laughed. "The inside is much better than the outside," he assured her. "Come on, I'll give you the VIP tour."

He turned and stepped back inside. After a moment, Mary heard a series of clicks, and to her delight the lights came on inside the school. "See, all the modern conveniences you could ask for," he said with a smile.

"That's much better," she said, stepping into the hallway. She started to say something else, but her words froze in her mouth when she heard a scream of terror and the sound of a body falling down the stairs.

Chapter Nine

"What?" Andrew asked, seeing the terrified look on Mary's face.

"Didn't you hear that scream?" she asked, not waiting for a response and hurrying down the hall towards the staircase. She arrived just in time to see a woman splayed across the top of the staircase, blood dripping from the crack in her skull, slowly disappear in front of her.

"Did you see her?" Andrew asked. "Did you see Miss Banks?"

Nodding slowly, Mary started up the stairs to where she'd seen the body. "Was this where they found her?" she asked.

"Yeah, this is the spot," he said. "Our classroom was just up the hall."

Mary took a deep, steadying breath. The body on the stairs had looked like she'd fallen backwards or had been pushed. Perhaps Andrew was right.

"Did they say how they thought it happened?" she asked.

He shrugged. "They said she must have had her arms full and didn't see the first step."

"But that doesn't explain her facing up position," Mary said.

"She wasn't facing up," Andrew said. "The police report says that the janitor found her facing down."

"Facing down?" Mary repeated.

Nodding, he climbed the stairs to the top. "They said that her feet were on the third step and she was facing down, her head against the railing," he said. "I got a copy of the report after I bought the school, just to see if I could find anything."

Mary shook her head. "Someone moved the body," she said. "I just saw what she looked like, and she was definitely facing up. Her feet might have still been up on the third step, but the fall was more like she stepped backwards onto the staircase."

"So, if someone moved the body..." he began.

She nodded. "At the very least, we know that someone was here when she died."

"Someone who wanted to disguise how she really died," Andrew inserted.

"Yeah," Mary agreed. "And most people don't need to disguise an accident."

She climbed up the remaining stairs and stood next to him. "But solving a crime after forty years with no suspects and no evidence isn't easy," she said.

"I don't want to give up," he said determinedly.

"Well, neither do I," she agreed. "I just want you to know that we've got a lot of work to do."

He sighed softly and nodded. "Okay, what's next?"

"Well, let's head over to the classroom and hope Miss Banks will show up and tell us who her killer was," Mary said. "That would make things so much easier."

Footsteps echoed in the empty school as they made their way past gray, metal lockers and bulletin boards with decade old notices on them. The doors to most of the classrooms were open, and Mary could see row after row of abandoned, wooden desks. The counters adjacent to the large windows were mostly empty, with an occasional book or discarded lunchbox on them.

Andrew led her to the fourth classroom. "Here we are," he said, entering the room first.

Mary walked through the doorway into the room and looked around at the small desks lined up in six rows. She walked slowly between the desks to the back of the class and imagined the woman she'd seen on the stairs moving between her students,

51

peering over their shoulders and checking on their progress. When she reached the back of the room, she turned and inhaled sharply. Standing next to Andrew in the front of the room was Miss Banks, her face bloodied and her body bruised.

"Are you Miss Banks?" Mary asked.

Andrew's eyes widened and he jumped to the side, looking at the empty space where Mary was directing her questions. "She's here?" he asked.

"Yes, I'm Kristen Banks," the ghost replied, her voice softly modulated and kind. "Are you here for one of my students?"

Mary glanced at Andrew. "She's here," she said to Andrew and then turned back to the ghost. "Actually, I'm a private investigator, and I'm here because one of your former students hired me."

Kristen smiled. "Well, I don't know how that would be possible," she said. "I've only been teaching for a few years, and I don't know many ten or eleven year olds who hire private investigators."

Mary slowly walked forward and stopped at the first desk in the row. She leaned against the desk that had been affixed to the floor and smiled at the ghost. "You made a great impression on him, you know," Mary said. "Your words on his spelling test made him finally believe in himself."

"Words on a spelling test?" Kristen said, shaking her head. "I'm afraid I don't understand."

"Andrew Tyler," Mary said. "Do you remember grading his spelling test?"

"Well, I do remember Andrew Tyler," she said. "But I just graded his test last night, so unless I'm Rip Van Winkle, I don't think you were hired by Andrew."

"Do you remember going home last night?" Mary asked.

Kristen stared at Mary. "Well, of course..." she began, pausing almost immediately. She looked up at Mary, her eyes wide and her face filled with concern. "I can't seem to remember..."

"Tell me what you do remember about last night," Mary urged.

"I was grading papers," she said slowly. "I'd just finished Andrew's paper, and then I took a moment to read Danny's letter." She looked up with an embarrassed smile. "Danny's my fiancé."

"Congratulations," Mary said. "Then what happened?"

Kristen paused for a moment while she searched her memory. "Then I heard a sound in the hall," she said slowly. "I got up and looked, but no one was there." She looked up at Mary again and

53

shrugged. "It kind of spooked me, so I decided to pack up and do the rest of the grading at home. I'm not very brave when it comes to those kinds of things."

"I guess you would have packed up your briefcase and your purse," Mary said, "and locked your classroom door?"

Kristen nodded. "Yes, I did," she said easily, but then her face fell and she looked down at the floor, studying it for a few minutes. When she looked up, her eyes were wide with horror. "He was there," she whispered, her voice shaky.

"Who?" Mary asked. "Who was there?"

"I don't know," she stammered. "He grabbed me from behind." She shuddered. "He touched me." Closing her eyes tightly, she wrapped her arms around herself. "He was...he was disgusting."

"What did you do?" Mary asked.

"He grabbed me," she said slowly, translucent tears sliding down her cheeks. "And he forced me to the stairs. He said he was going to take me." She looked up at Mary's eyes. "I had to get away."

"Yes. Yes, you did," Mary agreed.

"I kicked him," Kristen said, her voice breaking into sobs. "I kicked him, and he pushed me. He pushed me."

54

Wracked with sobs, tears flowing freely, she could barely speak. She took a deep, shuddering breath and looked at Mary, heart-breaking anguish in her eyes. "I fell," she whispered. "I fell, and I died."

Chapter Ten

"What happened?" Andrew asked, his eyes wide with curiosity and apprehension as he glanced around the room. "Is she still here?"

Mary shook her head, still staring at the empty space where Kristen had just stood. "No, she's gone now," she replied with a sigh.

"Why? Why did she leave?" he asked.

Taking a deep breath, Mary wiped the sadness from her eyes and turned to Andrew. "She just remembered what happened that night and comprehended that she was dead," she explained. "That's a fairly traumatic realization."

"What?" he asked. "She's been dead for over forty years. Why didn't she figure it out sooner?"

"Well, I don't have this all figured out perfectly yet," she said. "But it seems to me that often when death happens quickly, the spirits don't always understand they've passed on. They wake up in their spirit form and just keep repeating the actions from the life they lived."

"But forty years," he insisted. "Wouldn't she see that the faces in the classroom had changed? Wouldn't she notice that no one has been inside this school for a decade?"

"I'm not sure how cognizant they are of life around them," Mary said. "Sometimes it seems like their life is just a playback recording of what they did just before they died. So, perhaps in their mind, they see the things around them as if it were that day."

She shrugged. "It's not a perfect science," she admitted. "And I'm only putting together my own theories from the limited time I've spent with ghosts. Some of them are really aware they are dead and are trapped here until something gets resolved, but some are totally unaware of their situation. For them, the knowledge of their death generally comes as a big surprise. They keep living their life and going on with whatever was important to them when they died."

"So, does that mean she's gone? For good?" he asked.

"No," Mary replied, shaking her head and standing up. "It just means she needs a little time to deal with the reality of her situation. I'm sure now that she and I have met, she'll contact me. But until then, we just wait."

They both walked back to the hallway and stared at the staircase. "Did she know who did it?" he asked. "Did she remember who killed her?"

Turning to him, she met his eyes and sighed. "She never saw him," she explained. "Someone came up to her as she was leaving, grabbed her from behind and started forcing her towards the stairs. It sounded like it was supposed to have been an abduction or rape, but she fought back and he pushed her down the stairs."

"Rape?" he asked, incredulous. "This is Polo. People didn't get raped in Polo when I was a little kid. That just didn't happen."

Mary smiled sadly. "Oh, it happened," she said. "But victims didn't talk about it because they were ashamed or thought in some perverse way that it was their fault. So many rapists got away with it."

They started to walk towards the stairs. "Yeah, I understand how they wouldn't want to talk about it," he said. "Especially back then."

Mary stopped at the top of the staircase and turned to Andrew. "The problem with that secret is the darkness. Just like a drop of ink in water, it spreads throughout the rest of your life and darkens everything else," Mary replied. "Unless it's revealed, unless light is shone upon it, it doesn't go away."

They stood in silence for a moment, staring down at the steps. "So, how are we going to help Miss Banks?" he asked. "If she didn't see the man who did it, how can we possibly solve her murder?"

"Well, I guess we take it a step at a time," she said, and then she grimaced. "Excuse the horrible pun. I really didn't mean it."

Andrew actually smiled. "No problem," he said.

"Besides, we are closer to solving her murder," Mary said. "Because we finally know that it was a murder. And we wouldn't have known that if you hadn't saved the building."

They climbed down the stairs in silence, each lost in their own thoughts.

"Thank you, Mary, for coming out tonight," Andrew said when they reached the first floor and were walking towards the entrance, "even if we never see her again."

"You're welcome," she replied. "But don't give up; I'm sure we'll see her again. In the meantime, perhaps you could think of some people we could speak with who knew her and might know if she had an admirer."

"That's a great idea," he said. "Her parents are gone, but I can ask around and see if anyone remembers her and would be willing to talk. I have to admit, though, lately people in town aren't talking to me. I think some of them think I should leave the past in the past."

"They might be afraid," Mary warned. "Even though it was forty years ago, there's probably still a killer out there who doesn't want his secret revealed, and he might be willing to kill again just to be sure."

Andrew stopped in his tracks and looked at her. "You're right," he said. "I was so busy thinking about her, I really never thought that someone in our community is a cold-blooded killer."

Chapter Eleven

"The steps got closer, and the smell of blood was everywhere," Bradley said softly.

"You're doing better, but you have to say it like you're still there and you're really scared," Clarissa coached. Then she paused and looked at Bradley. "You were scared, weren't you?"

Bradley momentarily debated whether or not to protect his ego and lie or tell the truth. The truth won. "I was totally freaked out," he said with a smile. "I kept hearing footsteps, but I couldn't see anyone. I've never been so frightened in my life."

Clarissa clapped her hands together. "That's perfect, Daddy," she said. "You need to tell your story like that. You need to show how scared you were, and that will scare everyone else."

"You think?" he asked.

She shook her head eagerly. "Oh, yes, you actually even scared me that time," she said, holding out her arm. "See, I even have goosebumps."

Laughing, he leaned forward from his chair and ran his hand up her bare arm. "I see goosebumps," he confirmed. "But how about all those other times when you said you were frightened?"

She shrugged and slipped off the couch. "Oh, that was to help give you confidence," she replied with a smile, wrapping her arms around his neck and giving him a hug. "Now that you're actually good, you don't need it."

He gave her a hug and kissed her on the top of her head. "Thanks, coach," he said. "I feel better already."

"Did you ever actually see Earl?" she asked him.

"No, I never did," he said. "I heard him, and I smelled him." He scrunched up his nose. "And he smelled disgusting. But I never saw a ghost until Mary held my hand. Only then could I see them."

"That's good to know," she said. She leaned back in her father's arms and then slowly looked around the room. "Daddy, has anyone ever died in this house?" she asked.

Taken aback for a moment, Bradley shook his head and wondered why Clarissa would be asking a question like that. "No, sweetheart," he said, "Not that I know of. Why?"

"Just wondering," she said, squinting her eyes and slowly examining the room.

"Are you okay?" he asked.

She opened her eyes and nodded. "I'm great," she said. "Just checking."

"Checking for what?" he asked.

She sighed and shrugged. "Just checking," she said. "Where was Earl when he came into the house?"

Bradley pointed across the room to the basement door. "He was over there," he said.

"Cool," Clarissa said, wriggling out of Bradley's hold. She looked sideways, staring at the basement door from the corner of her eye and walked forward in the living room. Bradley grabbed her before she came into contact with the fireplace. "Sweetheart, you nearly bumped your head," he said. "Didn't you see the fireplace?"

She smiled up at him. "Oh, no, I didn't," she said. "Thanks for catching me, Dad."

He looked into her eyes. "Are your eyes okay?" he asked. "Is anything blurry?"

"No," she sighed. "Nothing's blurry. Everything looks just normal."

His brow furrowed in concern. He studied her for a few moments more and then placed another kiss on her head. "Okay, it's time for you to wash up and get ready for bed," he said. "Up you go."

She leaned forward and kissed his cheek. "Okay, Dad," she said. She turned and walked toward the staircase, her sideways gaze still locked on the area in front of the basement door. Suddenly she stumbled and fell forward on the staircase, but she was able to catch herself before she fell. Bradley was immediately at her side.

"Are you okay?" he asked.

"Sure," she replied carelessly. "I guess I just didn't see that step. Goodnight, Dad."

"Goodnight," he replied, concern in his voice.

He stood at the bottom of the stairway and watched her walk up, ready to catch her if she stumbled. What was going on with her? Was she having vision issues? Could she have cataracts, a detached retina or ...a tumor? His throat went dry, and his heart pounded in his chest. Could Clarissa be terminally ill?

He took a deep breath, ran his hand through his hair and leaned up against the bannister. Good grief, he needed to pull himself together. She stumbled and that was all. She was probably fine.

He stepped away from the staircase, then paused and looked up the stairs one more time. Well, just in case, he'd ask Mary what she thought.

Chapter Twelve

With a sincere feeling of gratitude, Mary parked her car close to the front of the superstore in a parking space saved for pregnant women. She knew the exercise of walking from the farther parts of the parking lot was good for her, but if she didn't hurry and get to the bathroom in the front of the store, she might embarrass herself. She hurried to the front of the store. She should have stopped at the gas station in Polo, she chided herself. When would she remember that her bladder currently had the capacity of less than a tablespoon?

A few minutes later, feeling much better about life, Mary took a cart from the cart corral and pushed it towards the seasonal section. As she approached, passing by the cards and gift-wrap section, she heard a familiar laugh. Turning her cart, she was surprised to see Kate and Rosie laughing together in the middle of the gift-wrap aisle. She glanced over at the cart and saw that the child's seat held two purses. They weren't just laughing together, they were shopping together.

"Hi," she said as she approached them, keeping her voice light. "Fancy meeting you here."

"Mary," Kate exclaimed, looking more surprised than she should. "What are you doing here?"

"Just picking up some Halloween candy for the school party," she replied. "Are you two shopping together?"

Rosie looked guiltier than Mary had ever seen. Were they embarrassed that they were out on the town without her? They always called her when they needed to go shopping, and they always shopped in a threesome.

Were they uncomfortable that they'd gone out shopping and hadn't called her? How many times had they done it? Had they even gone into Rockford without her? What? She wasn't a close enough friend anymore?

"We just ran into each other," Kate said.

But Mary knew it was a lie. You don't put your purse into a cart's child seat unless you are actually shopping together. That was the rule.

"Oh really?" Mary asked, keeping her tone friendly. "What a coincidence."

Rosie laughed nervously. "Yes. Yes it is quite a coincidence," she stammered. "First I run into Kate. Right, Kate? And then we both run into you." She waved her hand in front of her face nervously. "It probably looks like we are shopping together, but we're not. It's just as you said, a coincidence."

"Right, Rosie," Kate added and forced a quick laugh. "A coincidence, isn't that funny?"

"Yeah, hysterical," Mary replied, trying to keep the hurt from her voice. "But Rosie, I didn't see your car parked outside."

Rosie blanched. "Oh, I didn't drive here. Ka—, I mean, Stanley dropped me off. Yes, that's right. Stanley dropped me off and…." She looked confused for a moment and then turned to Mary with a wide smile on her face. "And he went over to the hardware store next door," she continued triumphantly. "He should be back soon, and then, of course, he'll drive me back home. Because I didn't come shopping with Kate. We just met here, er, coincidentally."

Mary's heart dropped. Her two best friends in the world on a shopping trip without her. It didn't matter if she already had made plans for the evening, they could have at least called and offered. Then she could have turned them down, and she would have known they weren't sneaking around being friends behind her back.

She slowly nodded at them, feeling at once betrayed and decidedly de trop. "Well, I'd better get that candy before it all sells out," she said. "Have fun shopping."

"We will," Kate replied. "By ourselves. I mean alone. I mean, each of us, not together, alone."

Mary nodded and smiled. "Right," she said.

Once Mary and her cart had traveled around the corner, Rosie breathed a sigh of relief. "I think that went well, don't you?" she asked Kate.

Shaking her head, Kate removed the handful of packages of paper tablecloths she'd thrown on top of the baby shower items as soon as she saw Mary walk into the aisle. "I don't know," Kate said. "I think she might have been suspicious."

"No," Rosie assured her. "I think we handled it really well."

"But we both had our purses in the child seat," Kate said.

"Oh, no," Rosie breathed softly. "Well, maybe she didn't see it. I was sort of standing in front of them."

Kate relaxed. "You're right," she said. "She probably never saw it. I guess I worry too much."

Rosie nodded. "Yes, you do," she said. "Besides, I could tell that she believed every word I said." She giggled. "I never knew I could be such an accomplished liar."

Mary stood in the adjacent aisle blatantly listening to their conversation and felt tears fill her eyes. She took a deep breath and angrily tossed a bag of candy into her cart. *Well, if they don't want to be my friends, fine,* she thought as she whipped another bag into her cart, *I don't need them anyway.*

Chapter Thirteen

Clarissa sat in her bed under her blankets with her arms wrapped around her knees. She knew she should have been sleeping, but she needed to talk to Mike.

"Okay, sweetheart, I think it's time for you to go to sleep," he said, hovering near her bedroom door.

"Can we talk for a minute?" she asked.

He turned away from the door and moved next to her bed. "Sure, what's up?"

"I'm kind of worried about Halloween. I have to have a good ghost story," she stalled, "or the rest of the O'Reillys will think I'm lame."

He shook his head and smiled down at her. "I don't think they would ever consider you lame," he said. "As a matter of fact, I have it on good authority that they think you are pretty awesome. But, I don't think that's why you wanted to talk to me, is it?"

She paused for a moment, looking down at her blankets, and then turned her face up to Mike again. "I figured something out today. I feel safe," she whispered. "Is that okay?"

"Sure, sweetheart, it's fine," he said, perching on the edge of the bed. "Why wouldn't you feel safe?"

Shaking her head, she sighed. "No, I don't mean it that way," she said, pausing to try and find the right words. "I finally feel safe. I finally feel like I don't have to worry anymore."

"Oh," he said, nodding slowly. "That kind of safe."

"Yeah," she said. "Am I? Should I feel this way?"

"So you're worried that you're not worried?" he teased, lifting an eyebrow over his left eye.

She giggled. "Kind of," she admitted.

"Let me ask you," he said. "What's your favorite kind of dessert?"

"Chocolate cake," she responded immediately.

"Very good choice," he said. "Okay, if you were sitting at the kitchen table downstairs and I put a huge piece of chocolate cake in front of you, what would you do?"

"Is this a trick question?" she asked.

"No," he said with a laugh. "It's a regular question. What would you do?"

"I'd eat it," she said.

"Would you enjoy it?"

"Yes."

"But wouldn't you be worried that every time you took a bite you got closer to not having any more cake?" he asked.

She shook her head. "No, that's silly," she said. "I have cake. Why worry about not having it."

"Exactly," he said. "You feel safe. You are loved, and your life is wonderful. Why would you worry about something in the future that may or may not happen? Why not enjoy your cake?"

She smiled up at him. "Are all guardian angels so smart?" she asked.

He leaned down and kissed her forehead. "No, sweetie, just me," he replied with a wink.

She giggled and scooted down into her blankets. "I love you, Mike."

"I love you, too," he said. "Now go to bed."

She rolled over on her side and closed her eyes. Soon she was sound asleep, and Mike watched her for a few more minutes before he faded away.

71

Chapter Fourteen

"Oh, good, you're home," Bradley said when Mary walked into the house thirty minutes later. "Do you need me to carry anything in from the car?"

Mary put two bags filled with candy and her purse on the table near the door and then turned to Bradley. "I saw Kate and Rosie at the store," she said, oblivious to his question.

"Well, that's nice," he replied, coming over to her. "How are they doing?"

"They were shopping," she said, and then she added meaningfully, "together."

She opened one of the bags and pulled out a plastic package of miniature chocolate candy bars, ripped open the top and picked one from the selection. Tearing open the wrapper, she bit viciously into the small confection. "They tried to deny it," she said, chewing ferociously. "But I could tell."

"Tell what?" Bradley asked, reaching over to grab of piece of candy for himself.

She absently pulled the bag to her side, her eyes wide with indignation. "Didn't you listen to what I said?" she asked. "They were shopping together."

She put her hand in, found another little candy victim, unwrapped it and bit it in half. "Together," she repeated, nodding angrily. "Not alone. Not a coincidence. Both purses in the child seat. They were together."

Yeah, this is definitely one of those woman things, Bradley thought, backing away as he watched Mary's sharp incisors decapitate yet another caramel-filled sweet. *Better just play along.*

"Well, that was certainly, uh…" he paused, praying for a little insight.

"Rude!" Mary finished for him. "Exactly. You are exactly right. That was just plain rude."

Thank you, God. Bradley sent up a quick prayer of silent thanks.

He smiled, feeling a little confident and nodded. "Yeah, that was rude," he said. "What the hell were they thinking? I mean really…"

He stopped talking and looked at Mary. She had a half-eaten candy in her hand and was staring at him with narrowed eyes. "Do you even know what they did?" she asked.

He felt his stomach twist. "They went shopping?" he said hesitantly.

"And do you know why I'm upset?" she asked, taking another quick bite of the candy.

"Because…" he said slowly, his palms sweating, "they should have…"

"Called me," she finished for him, waving her hand in the air. "Exactly. I mean, even you can understand that."

He wasn't about to ask her what she meant by even you, although he was pretty sure it wasn't a compliment.

She stopped waving her hands, dropped the bag of candy on the floor and started to cry. "They don't want to be my friends anymore," she sobbed.

He moved immediately, wrapping her in his arms and holding her. "Of course they do," he said. "Who wouldn't want to be your friend? You are amazing."

"But they went shopping without me," she cried against his shoulder.

"Maybe it was a last minute thing," he said. "Maybe they saw that your car was gone and figured you had to work."

She looked up at him and sniffed. "Are you taking their side?" she asked.

He pulled her back into his arms quickly. "No. No, of course not," he said. "But they've both done so much for us; I wanted to give them the benefit of the doubt."

She nodded slowly. "That's true," she said, her voice muffled in his shirt. "They really have done a lot. And maybe I'm making too much out of it. The doctor did warn me that my hormones might go crazy, and I might be experiencing bouts of emotional highs and lows."

"That's true," Bradley said softly.

She pulled back and stared at him. "So, you think that I'm making this whole thing up?" she asked angrily. "That my two so-called best friends can go shopping with each other and not invite me. And this is all my hormones' fault?"

I'm dead, Bradley thought, *just kill me right now.*

He looked down at his wife, her eyes red-rimmed and slightly swollen from crying, a little bit of chocolate and caramel on her lips and her hair slightly mussed from his arms. She was the most beautiful thing in the world.

Then he thought about Rosie and Kate. He knew they were shopping for Mary's baby shower, knew that all of the secrecy was only because they loved her. He could end all of Mary's misery by just telling her the truth, by telling her that her dear friends were going to surprise her in a few days, by telling her that she had nothing to worry about. He sighed. He would totally spoil the surprise they'd been working on for weeks.

75

He thought about what they would want him to do, and realizing the truth, he slid his hands to Mary's shoulders and looked down into her eyes.

"Those witches," he breathed and watched her face break into a radiant smile, like the sunshine after a rainstorm.

"Thank you, Bradley," she said with a soft shudder. "It's so nice to have a husband who understands."

He pulled her back into his arms and exhaled with relief. *Only three more months to go.*

Chapter Fifteen

"Good morning," Clarissa said sleepily as she made her way down the stairs the next morning.

"Morning, sweetheart," Mary replied with a smile. "You look tired."

Rubbing her eyes, Clarissa nodded. "Uh-huh," she mumbled as she climbed onto her chair next to the kitchen table. Then she yawned widely. "I am."

Mary filled a bowl with oatmeal, sprinkled raisins, dried cranberries and brown sugar on it and brought it over to the table. She set it down in front of her daughter and slipped into the chair next to her.

"Is anything wrong?" she asked, placing her hand on Clarissa's forehead to check for a fever.

Clarissa reached across the table for the pitcher of milk and poured some over her cereal. She shook her head. "No, I stayed up late. Checking," she yawned.

"Checking for what?" Mary asked.

Clarissa spooned a small portion of oatmeal into her mouth. "For ghosts," she replied, her words garbled around the food. She swallowed and then looked up at Mary. "Did anyone ever die in this house?"

Mary thought about it for a moment and then shook her head. "Sorry, no," she said. "No one died here. It's a peaceful house." She paused for a moment. "Well, except when I have company."

"Maggie says that if you look sideways you can see ghosts," she said, demonstrating the sideways look to Mary.

Mary choked back a chuckle. "Well, actually, Maggie is right, sort of," she replied.

"Sort of?" Clarissa asked.

"Well, scientists have studied our eyes, and they have found that the corners of our eyes are more sensitive to light and movement," she explained. "So, often we can see paranormal things, like ghosts, in the corners of our eyes, but when we turn and view them with full vision, they might disappear."

"But they're still there?" Clarissa asked.

Mary shrugged and nodded. "They could be," she said. "But looking for ghosts out of the corners of your eyes can cause some other troubles."

Clarissa sighed. "I know," she said, absently rubbing her forehead. "Like walking into bookshelves."

"Exactly," she said. "I had a ghost investigator from Chicago tell me that I should just try to be aware of my surroundings. Then, if I saw something out of the corner of my eye, I should try to keep watching it that way and not quickly turn towards it."

"Do ghosts want to be seen?" Clarissa asked.

"Sometimes," Mary said. "And sometimes not. I think when they have a problem or need help, they want to be seen. But sometimes they are just visiting some of the places that were special to them when they were alive, so they are just on a walk."

Clarissa giggled. "Hello, I'm just a ghost on a walk," she teased, lowering her voice. "Please don't look at me."

Mary laughed. "Exactly," she said, and then she lowered her voice, too. "Hello, I'm a ghost on a walk. Can you tell me the way to the nearest bootique?"

"Do you know where I can buy a halloweenie for lunch?" Clarissa added with a laugh.

"Knock, knock," Mary continued.

"Who's there?" Clarissa replied.

"Boo."

"Boo who?" Clarissa answered, her eyes sparkling with mirth.

"Oh, sorry, didn't mean to scare you and make you cry," Mary finished.

Bradley exhaled with relief when he heard the laughter coming up the stairs to greet him. It was going to be a normal day in the Alden household. He stopped on the stairs and checked that thought. It was going to be as normal as possible.

"Good morning my beautiful ladies," he said as he came into the kitchen. "What's up?"

Clarissa hopped out of her chair, threw her arms around him and gave him a kiss. "Hello, I'm a ghost on a walk, and I have to get ready for school," she announced, and then she ran up the stairs to her bedroom.

So much for normal, Bradley thought.

He turned to his wife. "Could you explain that?" he asked.

"What?" she replied, looking completely befuddled.

"Clarissa is a ghost on a walk, and she has to get ready for school," he repeated.

She stopped in the process of filling a bowl of oatmeal for Bradley and looked at the clock on the wall. "She's right," she replied. "It is time for her to get ready. Good for her."

Bradley took the offered bowl and shook his head. *Okay, I'm going to try again.*

He sat down at the table and started pouring milk over his oatmeal. "Mary," he began. "I'm a little worried about Clarissa's eyesight. Last night she kept walking into things, but she said everything was fine."

Walking over to Bradley, Mary chuckled and bent over to kiss his cheek. "She is just adorable, isn't she?" she asked with a grin and walked towards the stairs.

"But, aren't you worried?" he asked.

She shook her head. "No," she replied hurriedly. "I told her no one died in this house, so it's okay."

He watched her walk up the stairs, his face a study in confusion. Finally, he sighed, took a deep breath and stuck his spoon in his oatmeal. *I give up.*

Chapter Sixteen

Mary sat back in her chair and stretched. Looking around her desk, she could see the remains of the morning's snacks: string cheese wrappers, an empty yogurt carton, and, she wasn't proud of it, a still half-filled snack-sized bag of Oreos. She'd been in the office for about an hour and a half, had finished her correspondence, and was now going to start doing some research on Kristen Banks. She typed her name into the search engine and paused. *Nope. First I'm going to the bathroom,* she decided, *and then I'll look for Miss Banks.*

A few minutes later, as she returned from the bathroom towards her desk, she was more than a little surprised to see Kristen Banks peering into her computer screen on her desk. "Hello?" Mary asked softly. "Were you looking for me?"

Kristen turned, her face still blood-stained and battered, her expression one of confusion and interest. "What's that?" she asked, pointing to the computer.

"That's my laptop," Mary replied.

"No," Kristen said, slapping her hands to her thighs. "This is a laptop. That looks like a miniature television."

Mary smiled and walked back to her chair, slipping around Kristen and sitting down. "Actually, things have changed a little since you died," she explained to the ghost. "Do you remember hearing about computers?"

Kristen thought for a moment. "Yes," she said. "The government used them for the space program, and some corporations use them."

"Well, this is one of them," Mary said. "Actually, this one has more power than the ones that NASA used to run the Apollo mission."

Kristen looked at the small laptop and then back at Mary. "That can't be true," she said. "It's so tiny."

"It's amazing how technology has grown over the years," she said. "I have a phone that can text, answer emails and search the internet."

Kristen stared at Mary. "I'm sorry, what?" she asked.

Mary opened her mouth to explain but decided against it. "It does a lot of cool stuff," she improvised. "But, let's get back to you. I'm so glad you came to see me."

"I actually hadn't planned to come," Kristen admitted. "But I thought about what happened last night and ,poof, I ended up here. So, who are you?"

"Well, I guess the best way to describe it is that I'm a private investigator who works with ghosts," Mary said.

"Like the Rockford Files?" Kristen asked.

Mary quickly typed 'Rockford Files' in her search engine and saw the description of the 1970s private investigator show. "Yes, exactly," she said. She looked at the photos. "And James Garner was a hunk."

Kristen smiled. "I always thought so," she said. "So, what was that you did? Typing in the information?"

"That's called a search engine," she said. "You can type in a name or a question and get information about it from all around the world."

"Does it find people? I mean real people, not just celebrities?" she asked, leaning closer.

"It can," Mary replied.

"Could you find my fiancé? Danny, I mean Daniel Toba?" she said.

"I can try," Mary said, typing the name into the search engine and adding Polo, Illinois. She clicked enter, and the top result was a social networking page. "I think I found him."

She clicked on the page, and immediately a photo of a fairly portly, bald-headed man in his sixties showed up.

"He's old," Kristen exclaimed, staring at the photo. "And he's fat."

"Well, it been forty years since you last saw him," Mary replied.

"How could he let himself go like that?" she asked her face filled with disgust. Then she turned to Mary and, placing her hands on her hips, shook her head slowly. "It was probably the grief, wasn't it? He came home and found out I was dead, and he just...he just went to hell."

Mary clicked on his information. "Well, he eventually did get married," she said.

"What?" Kristen exclaimed. "He got married?"

Mary skimmed over the information and then bit her lower lip.

"What?" Kristen demanded. "I taught school for enough time to know when someone's hiding the truth."

"He got married about a year after you died," Mary admitted.

"A year? Well, obviously he meant more to me than I did to him," she snapped.

"Maybe it was a rebound kind of thing," Mary suggested.

Kristen wasn't buying it. "Who did he marry?" she asked.

Mary clicked on his photos and found his spouse. "It looks like he married Janice."

"Janice?" she cried, backing away from Mary's desk. "He knew I hated Janice. How could he marry Janice?"

"It looks like they had three lovely children," Mary inserted.

Kristen walked back to the desk and peered over Mary's shoulder. "Well, did they at least name one of them Kristen?" she asked.

Mary shook her head. "No, it doesn't…"

"Wait a minute," Kristen cried, reading over Mary's shoulder. "Their dog? Their dog!" She walked to the middle of the room and screamed, the haunting sound echoing off the walls. "They named their damned dog after me!"

She disappeared in a puff, and Mary just stared at the empty space for a few minutes. Then she turned back to look at the computer screen, picked up the bag of Oreos and stuffed one in her mouth. "Well, it's a cute dog," she murmured.

Chapter Seventeen

"So, I guess we got ourselves a celebrity visiting our little town," Dale Epperly said as he walked into the small café in the downtown area.

"What's that you say?" George Willingford called out from across the room.

"I said we got ourselves a celebrity," Dale shouted back, knowing that George was not only hard-of-hearing but also always seemed to forget his hearing aid when he left his home.

"You need some celery?" George asked. "Why don't you go down to the market?"

"He said we have a celebrity in town," Vivian Kutchens, the owner of the restaurant, said. There was something about the tenor of Viv's voice that somehow penetrated George's hearing problem, and he heard her right away.

"Well, you don't say," he said. "Some kind of movie star?"

Dale walked over to the counter and slipped into a seat. "Naw, nothing like that," he said, reaching for the cup of coffee Viv poured him. "Just that gal who was in the paper the other day. The one that says she can see ghosts."

Viv nodded slowly. "Don't you make fun of that, Dale Epperly," she said as she wiped down the counter in front of Dale. "I've seen things that would make you shake in your boots."

"Yeah, Dale and she ain't just talking about your wife without makeup on," George teased.

"Oh, really, George?" she asked. "Seems I remember a story you used to tell about seeing a ghost back by your barn a couple of summers ago."

George paused and shrugged. "Guess you're right," he said. "Somehow I forgot it."

"Forgot what?" another voice asked as the door to the café opened. "George, you forget your hearing aid again?"

"Hey, Mitch," Viv said. "Have a seat. No, George just remembered he shouldn't be making fun of the lady in town who says she sees ghosts."

Mitchell Howse slid his large frame into the corner chair at the counter, giving himself a little more room. "What lady?" he asked, absently picking up the menu.

"That lady in the paper a while back," Dale said, his voice heavy with skepticism. "The one that solves mysteries 'cause she can talk to dead people. I seen her out at the old school last night."

Mitchell slowly put the menu back in the holder and turned to Dale. "What the hell is she doing out at the old school?" he asked, keeping his voice low.

Dale shrugged. "Well, my guess would be, seeing that it was night time and the place is empty, that she's on a ghost hunt," he laughed.

"That place is dangerous," Mitch growled, "Should have been torn down a long time ago. Who the hell let her go in?"

He looked accusingly around the room and scowled. "I thought the city council voted to condemn that place," Mitch continued. "I'm sure they voted on it months ago."

"Yeah, they did," George replied. "I read it in the paper. But now they got to go to a judge and get things all worked out."

"How long does that take?" Mitch asked.

George shrugged. "Don't know," he said. "The wheels of justice never seem to hurry themselves around. Could be another year before they get around to it."

"Besides," Dale said. "it ain't like she's going to find anything in there. The only person who died in that school was that young teacher. What was her name?"

"Christine," George said. "It was Christine."

"No, it was Kristen," Viv inserted, pushing a cup of coffee to Mitch. "Kristen Banks. As I recall, she tripped down the stairs."

"I don't suppose ghosts haunt a place because they were clumsy," Dale said. "That would be almost embarrassing for them."

Mitch slid out of the chair. "Sorry, Viv," he said, pushing the coffee cup away and putting down a couple of dollars. "I just remembered something I had to do."

Chapter Eighteen

"Mrs. Spangler?" Clarissa asked, looking up at her fourth grade teacher.

"Yes, Clarissa," Mrs. Spangler replied, placing her hand softly on Clarissa's shoulder.

Clarissa loved the way Mrs. Spangler answered questions. She put her hand on your shoulder and looked right into your eyes, like your question was the most important thing in the world.

Clarissa smiled up at her. "Do you know if anyone ever died in our classroom?"

Mrs. Spangler's smile faltered just a bit, but then she regained it. "Why no, Clarissa," she said. "I'm afraid I don't have any information about that. Why did you want to know?"

Clarissa shrugged. "I was just wondering," she replied.

Knowing about some of the frightening circumstances when Clarissa was younger, the concerned teacher pressed a bit further. "Are you afraid of something?" she asked. "Are you worried someone might die?"

Shocked, Clarissa shook her head. "No, I'm not," she replied, her voice hesitant. "Are you?"

"No. No, of course not," Mrs. Spangler assured her. "I just thought you were worried."

"No," Clarissa said casually. "I was just wondering. That's all."

"Oh. Well, that's fine then," the teacher said, patting Clarissa's shoulder gently. "I'm sorry I couldn't be of more help."

"That's okay," the child replied frankly. "If I find out about any, I'll let you know."

Mrs. Spangler watched the little girl walk out of the classroom accompanied by her best friend, Maggie Brennan, and shook her head. It was funny how the slightly peculiar children seemed to be drawn to each other. And those two were certainly peas from the same pod.

"What did you ask Mrs. Spangler?" Maggie asked Clarissa as they walked towards the curb where Kate's minivan was waiting.

Clarissa shrugged. "Oh, nothing. I just asked her if anyone had ever died in the classroom."

Stopping in the middle of the sidewalk, Maggie shook her head at her friend. "You know, you're not supposed to do that," she said. "It kind of freaks people out."

"I didn't know that," Clarissa said. "Why?"

Maggie sighed. "Clarissa, most people don't believe in ghosts," she said. "It makes them uncomfortable to talk about dead people."

Eyes widening in understanding, Clarissa nodded to her friend. "Well no wonder she looked so surprised," she said. "So, is this like a secret?"

"It's kind of like a family secret," she explained. "Like you can tell your mom and dad, 'cause they get it. But everyone else probably thinks you're nuts."

"But Mrs. Spangler just read us a bunch of ghost stories," Clarissa argued.

"But she thinks they're just *stories*," Maggie replied.

"Ohhhhhh," Clarissa said. "She doesn't know they're real? But I thought she was real smart."

"Nope," Maggie said. "My mom says she's not stupid or anything. She's just ignorant."

"Ohhh," Clarissa replied, nodding. Then she paused for a moment. "Um, Maggie?"

"Yeah," Maggie said as they continued toward the minivan.

"What does ignorant mean?"

Maggie paused again and then turned to her friend. "I think it means stupid, but it's nicer. Kind of like shut up and be quiet."

"Oh, okay," Clarissa replied easily. "Come on, I'll race you the rest of the way."

The girls took off, laughing and screaming, as they raced to the curb.

"Whoa, slow down there," Kate Brennan said, catching the girls in a hug. "How was your day?"

"Great," Maggie said. "Rusty threw up again in school."

Clarissa nodded. "Right after lunch, so it was huge."

"Is he okay?" Kate asked.

The girls nodded casually. "Yeah, he throws up whenever there's a math test," Maggie explained. "His mother told the teacher that he has math 'xiety."

"You mean anxiety?" Kate asked.

"Does anxiety make you throw up?" Clarissa asked.

Kate smiled. "Sometimes."

"Then that must be it," Clarissa said, climbing into the van.

"So, Clarissa, how's your mom doing today?" Kate asked.

"She's fine," Clarissa answered absently.

"Was she happy this morning?" Kate continued, worried she had hurt her friend's feelings the night before.

"Yes, she was really happy," Clarissa said, "because we were talking about ghosts and she's not ignorant."

"Well, good," Kate replied, slightly confused. "That's really good to hear."

Chapter Nineteen

"We're going to look at some books over there," Maggie said to her mother once they arrived at the library.

"Okay," Kate said. "But we can't be very long today. I have a lot to do."

"We'll hurry, Mom," Maggie said, grabbing Clarissa's hand. "We promise."

They wound their way around the tall stacks of books to the far corner and then hurried to the desk.

Clarissa looked down the dark aisle. "The books aren't moving," she whispered. "Is he gone today?"

Maggie shook her head. "He's not by the books. He's by the window today," she said. "He's just looking outside."

Clarissa turned her head so she could look sideways towards the window. She focused for a few moments and then sighed. "All I see is blur," she said. "I've been practicing all day and all last night, and all I see is blur."

"I don't know what else to try," Maggie confessed.

"When Mary touches my dad, he can see ghosts like she does," Clarissa suggested.

Maggie reached over and held Clarissa's hand, and suddenly Clarissa saw the tall man standing next to the window, gazing outside with his hands clasped behind his back. The girls stood together, silently watching him for a few moments. He looked so thoughtful. Clarissa tugged on Maggie's hand. "Maybe we should go," she whispered. "He looks sad."

Maggie was just about to answer when he turned his head and saw them. His long, wrinkled face seemed to light up, and he smiled down at them.

He turned to Maggie. "Hello, Miss Maggie," he said, offering her a proper bow. "How are you this afternoon?"

Maggie grinned up at him. "I am fine, sir," she replied. "Thank you very much. This is my friend Clarissa."

He bowed to her, too. "Hello, Miss Clarissa," he said. "What kind of books do you like to read?"

Clarissa shrugged. "I like all kinds," she said. "I used to like only the books with pictures, but now I like the ones with lots of words, too. Middle graders."

"Middle graders?" the man asked. "I don't know what those are."

97

"Oh, they're books for kids in the middle grades, like third and fourth grade," she explained. "That's why I like them."

She studied him for a moment. He looked a little familiar, like she'd seen him before. "Do you live in Freeport?" she asked.

He shook his head. "No, but I come to visit quite often," he said. "Why?"

"You look like I know you," she replied.

Smiling, he nodded. "I've been told that before," he said. "I must have one of those faces that people find familiar."

"Are there those kinds of faces?" she asked.

He shrugged. "There must be, because I have one," he replied with a grin.

She laughed softly. "What kinds of stories do you like?" she asked.

"Oh, I like many stories," he said. "But my favorites, when I was your age, were Aesop's Fables."

Maggie crinkled up her nose in confusion. "What are those?" she asked.

"They are wonderful stories that teach lessons," he said. "The most well-known was about a race between a tortoise and a hare."

"Oh, I know that one," Clarissa replied with an excited smile. "I just didn't know it was a... a sop fable."

Aesop's Fable," the man replied gently.

"I'd like to hear you tell us one," Maggie said. "But we don't have much time. My mom has a lot to do today."

He nodded. "Leave nothing for tomorrow which can be done today," he said. "You never know what the future will bring."

"What does that mean?" Clarissa asked.

He stepped away from the window and pulled out two of the chairs at the desk. "Would you join me for a few moments?" he asked.

Clarissa slipped up onto the chair, and Maggie climbed onto the other. As soon as Clarissa let go of Maggie's hand, she realized the ghost disappeared, so she quickly reached over and took Maggie's' hand once again. Once the girls were situated, he sat across from them. "So, you want me to explain my wise words?" he asked, a twinkle in his eyes.

Clarissa nodded. "Yes sir," she said. "If you don't mind."

"Well, leave nothing for tomorrow which can be done today means that you should not put off your responsibilities, but do them right away," he explained.

Clarissa sighed. "I thought you might have meant something like that," she said. "That's something grownups always say."

He chuckled softly. "Well, perhaps we say it because we have put things off ourselves and then regretted it later."

"I can't wait until I become an adult and then I can tell kids what to do," Maggie said. "My mom tells us what to do all the time."

"The best thing about the future is that it comes one day at a time," he said.

"You talk funny," Clarissa said.

He laughed out loud and nodded. "Yes, I do believe I do," he agreed, and then he leaned forward. "Can I tell you a secret?"

They nodded eagerly.

"When I was a little boy, I had a terrible stutter when I spoke," he said. "It took me a long time to learn how to speak properly."

Clapping her hands over her mouth, Clarissa was immediately contrite. "Oh, I'm so sorry," she said and then quickly grabbed her friend's hand so the ghost would reappear. "I didn't mean to make you sad."

He smiled at her and shook his head. "But, you didn't," he said. "And neither has anyone else who criticized my speech throughout my life." He winked at her. "Because I knew my secret, and they didn't."

"Thank you for sharing your secret with us," Clarissa said.

He nodded. "Well, of course, secrets are not much fun unless they're shared."

Maggie's eyes widened, and she nodded eagerly. "That's what I think," she said. "What good's a secret if you can't tell someone?"

He chuckled. "Well, you just have to be sure to share them with the right people," he warned.

"Are you the right people?" Clarissa asked.

"I believe you can trust me with your secrets," he replied. "And I am all ears."

Clarissa looked at the side of his face and nodded. "They are pretty big," she acknowledged.

He chuckled again. "Yes, I've been told that, too," he replied.

"Maggie is trying to help me see ghosts," Clarissa said.

He sat back in his chair and ran his hand over his beard. "You don't say," he said. "Doesn't that frighten you? Most children are afraid of death."

"My real mommy was a ghost," Clarissa explained. "And now she's an angel."

The man nodded and reached across the desk to enfold the child's hand. It felt like a cold puff of air around her hand. "I understand the pain of losing your mother when you are a child," he said. "All that I was, or hoped to be, I owe to my angel mother."

"I like you," Clarissa said. "You're not scary at all."

He stood and bowed to her. "I like you, too," he said. "I hope we have the opportunity to meet again."

"Maggie, Clarissa, where are you?" Kate's whispered voice came from around the corner of the book shelf.

Clarissa turned and looked behind her. "It's your mom," she whispered to Maggie. "Can she see…"

She turned back, but the man was gone.

"He does that," Maggie whispered. "I don't think he likes big people."

"I liked him," Clarissa said, getting out of the chair and walking toward the book shelf. "I can't believe he's a ghost. He's so nice."

Maggie nodded, walking alongside her friend. "Lots of ghosts are nice," she said, "but people are usually too scared to find out."

"Thanks for letting me meet your friend," Clarissa said. "But I don't know if he's scary enough to be my Halloween story."

Chapter Twenty

Mary absently picked up a few more kernels of buttered popcorn as she clicked on the screen with her mouse. She had been accessing vital records from Ogle County and wasn't getting anywhere. Her next stop was the newspaper archives, and she hoped they had them online. As she clicked on the next record, she put the popcorn in her mouth and reached for another few kernels.

"Do you really think you should be eating that?"

Dropping the popcorn back into the bowl, Mary quickly turned to see that Kristen had reappeared in her office. "I beg your pardon?" she asked the ghost.

Kristen moved closer to the desk. "I really hate to be rude," she began, taking a moment to pointedly look at Mary's stomach. "But, really, you don't need popcorn."

Taking a deep breath, Mary decided her best option would be to not react to Kristen's comment. "Welcome back," she said. "I'm glad the information on your former fiancé didn't keep you away."

Shrugging, Kristen glided across the room and looked over Mary's shoulder at her computer screen. "Oh, well, after seeing his new look, I figured I really dodged a bullet on that one," she replied. "But that doesn't mean I don't want to find the guy who killed me. I mean, I was a fourth grade teacher. Who kills a fourth grade teacher?"

"I was just looking over some records, and even though there are a lot of accidental deaths, I really don't see anything that seems to be related to your murder," Mary explained.

"You're really nothing like the Rockford files are you?" Kristen asked. "I mean, a fat private investigator who sits in her office and eats popcorn all day is really not exciting television, is it?"

"However, a rude, self-centered ghost might become a movie of the week," Mary muttered.

"Excuse me?" Kristen asked. "Are you criticizing the dead girl?"

Mary took a deep breath. "Okay, sweetheart, I've had just about enough of you," Mary said, letting her pregnant hormones take over. "You were killed over forty years ago. And now that I've gotten to know you a little, maybe I can see why. Although, I'm really surprised anyone thought it was an accident. I'm sure you had plenty of people out for your blood."

"Everyone loved me!" Kristen yelled. "I was up for teacher of the year. They don't just give that away to anyone."

"Well, teacher of the year," Mary shouted back, "maybe you should have tried for Miss Congeniality, and then you wouldn't be dead."

"I never said anything mean to anyone!" Kristen screamed back. "I only wrote that kind of stuff in my journal."

"Maybe someone found your journal and read it," Mary yelled back.

"No, it was in a secret compartment," Kristen exclaimed. "I'm not stupid."

"A secret compartment?" Mary asked.

Kristen shrugged. "Yeah, well, some of the stuff I wrote about my colleagues and the principal could have gotten me fired," she said. "I guess I can be pretty blunt."

"Really?" Mary replied sarcastically. "What a surprise."

Just then the front door to Mary's office opened, and the bell rang. "Well, hello there," Kristen purred, looking over Mary's shoulder to the front of the office. "Now that's what I call Officer Tall, Dark and Handsome. Honey, you can arrest me anytime."

Mary spun her chair around and saw Bradley walking toward her desk. "Hi," she said.

He leaned over her desk and kissed her. "Hi yourself," he replied.

"So, he likes fat girls?" Kristen asked, floating over next to the desk. "What a waste."

"I'm not fat. I'm pregnant," Mary replied through gritted teeth.

Bradley looked at her questioningly. "Yeah, I know," he said. "And you're not just pregnant, you're ravishing."

"Oh, so he's the one who got you knocked up," Kristen stated. "Lucky you."

With a long-suffering sigh, Mary placed her hand on Bradley's arm and said, "Bradley, I want you to meet Kristen Banks, a former fourth-grade teacher. Kristen, this is my *husband*, Bradley."

With Mary's touch, Bradley was able to see the ghost of the young woman standing next to Mary's desk. He had to admit it was still a little disconcerting to be able to see dead people, but he was getting used to it.

"Hello, Kristen," he said.

She studied him for a moment. "Do you think you're going to get fat?" she asked.

Concern crossed over Bradley's features. He looked down at his waistline and looked back at the ghost. "Why do you ask?"

Shrugging, she sighed. "Well, I had a fiancé who looked a lot like you when we were engaged," she said. "He was a real hunk. But I just saw a picture of him, and he's pretty much gone to hell. I just wondered if all hunks turn out that way."

"You think I'm a hunk?" Bradley asked, a grin spreading across his face. He looked down at Mary and nodded in Kristen's direction. "She thinks I'm a hunk."

Mary bit back a smile. "Yeah, I heard," she said. "And I agree."

"I wasn't trying to compliment you," Kristen interrupted. "I just wanted to know if you were going to get fat."

"I'm not planning on it," Bradley said. "But thanks for asking."

"You two deserve each other," Kristen snapped. "But what did I do to deserve ending up haunting McMillan and wife for the rest of eternity?"

"Who?" Mary asked.

Kristen threw her hands up in the air. "I'm doomed."

"Mary will help you cross over," Bradley said. "She always does."

Sighing heavily, Kristen shook her head. "The only clues we might have are in my journal, and unless my old desk is still around, that journal is long gone. So, we can't find anyone."

Mary stopped and shook her head. "Wait. What? Your old desk?"

"Yes. My old desk. Because that's where the secret compartment was," Kristen said slowly, as if Mary wasn't very smart. "In my desk."

Chapter Twenty-one

"I'm so glad you're here," Mary said when Andrew opened the door to the old school. "Kristen stopped by my office and told me about a possible clue."

"Great," Andrew said, looking around the hall. "Where is it?"

"In her classroom," Mary said, heading in that direction. "But let's hurry. I'd rather not turn on the lights and let the neighbors know we're here."

Mary started dashing up the stairs, but after the first ten steps, she realized that she just couldn't dash anymore. Grasping the handrail, she stopped to catch her breath and then continued up in a more sedate pace. "I keep forgetting I'm pregnant," she breathlessly apologized.

"Oh, no, don't worry," Andrew said. "We have plenty of time. We can go slower if you'd like."

Mary smiled at him. "I'm good, thank you," she said. "We don't need to go slower."

They reached the second floor and walked down the hallway to the classroom. Mary hurried to the desk and pulled open the top drawer on the right side. "She said there was a secret compartment in the drawer," Mary said, knocking on the bottom of the drawer.

"You're kidding." he exclaimed, looking over her shoulder. "I swear I checked this desk inside and out."

Mary stopped searching and looked at him. "You already searched the desk?" she asked.

"Yeah," he said. "I did everything I could to solve the mystery myself. I got the police report. I went through the school records, and I searched throughout the whole school." He chortled lightly. "If I hadn't read the article about you, I'd still be…"

Mary's blood ran cold. "You read the article about me?" she asked.

He nodded. "Yeah, that's why I came to see you," he said. "Why else would you think…"

"Mary!"

Mary looked up to see Mike standing in the middle of classroom. "Mike?"

"You need to get out of here," he said, his voice tense. "I can't interfere, but danger is coming."

"Mike? Who's Mike?" Andrew asked.

She held her hand up to silence him. She heard a noise outside the classroom door.

"Andrew, we need to leave the school right away," she said, yanking out the drawer and tucking it under her arm. "I need you to meet me at my house. And then we need to talk. Can you do that?"

"What?" Andrew asked. "What's wrong?"

"We just need to get out now," she said. "And you need to promise that you'll come to my house."

"I promise," Andrew said, his voice shaking. He looked around the room. "Are we going to be okay?"

"I sure hope so," Mary said.

She walked over to the window and surreptitiously looked down to the parking lot. As far as she could see, no one was out there. But, she reasoned, a killer would not park their car in plain view. She turned and realized Andrew had already left. Taking a deep breath, she hurried to the classroom door and carefully opened it so it didn't make any noise. She slowly stuck her head out and looked up and down the hallway.

"Looking for something?" Kristen asked, appearing behind Mary.

Mary jumped back and stifled a scream. Her heart in her throat, she turned back to the ghost. "Do you remember the night you died?" she asked.

Kristen's haughty face dropped, and fear shone on it. "Yes, I do," she said, her voice low.

"I'm afraid that the same person who murdered you might be here in the school tonight," Mary said. "And he might be looking for his next victim."

Kristen backed up against the wall of the classroom next to the door. "We can't go out there, Mary," she said, her voice trembling with terror. "He's going to get us."

Mary clicked the lock closed on the inside of the door. "Well, I don't think we can stay here for much longer," she replied. "It's getting darker, and I won't be able to make it down the stairs."

"We should call the police," Kristen suggested.

"He might be the police," Mary said.

"Oh, I hadn't thought of that," she replied.

"Kristen, can you move that chair?" Mary asked.

"Why? Do you need to sit down?" she asked.

"No, I just need to see if you can move things."

Kristen walked next to the desk and pushed on the chair. It moved several feet.

113

"Oh, that's great," Mary said. "Is there another exit in the school?"

"Yeah, the front exit," Kristen replied. "There's another set of stairs in the other direction that lead to the front exit."

"Okay, I want you to go in that direction, and when you get close to the other set of stairs, make as much noise as you can," Mary said. "Push trash cans or chairs or whatever down the stairs, and then you can leave."

"But what about you?"

"As soon as I hear someone running after you, I'll head down the other stairs and get out," she said.

Kristen took the drawer away from Mary, pressed on the hidden lock, and slid open the panel revealing her journal and the letters. "Take these," she said. "It will be much easier for you to just carry them, and I'll use this drawer as the first thing to go down the stairs."

"Thank you, Kristen," Mary said, turning and unlocking the door. "Good luck."

"Yeah, you, too," Kristen replied, opening the door and slipping outside with the drawer in her hands.

Mary slid against the wall, the classroom door slightly ajar next to her, and waited. Finally, she heard the sound of the drawer bouncing down the stairs, and then she heard footsteps coming from just down the hall from her. She held her breath and prayed.

Her heart jumped when she heard the footsteps pause next to the door, but another clatter on the stairs had them starting up again. She counted to five and then dashed out of the room and the other way down the hall. Grasping the handrail tightly, she flew down the stairs as quickly as she could, her breath caught in her throat. Finally, she reached the main floor and ran down the hall towards the door. She pushed open the door and ran towards her car, clicking the automatic unlock when she was five steps away.

She pulled open the door, jumped inside and shoved the key into the ignition. A moment later she had pulled out of the parking lot and was speeding down the street. She reached into her purse, pulled out her phone and called Bradley.

"Hey, honey," he said. "How are you—"

"Bradley," she sobbed. "I'm on my way home, and I need you to see if Clarissa can go over to Maggie's tonight."

"Honey, what's wrong?" he asked.

"I'll tell when I get home," she said. "But I'm afraid I've just stumbled into a recent murder."

Chapter Twenty-two

The beams from the headlights of Mary's car flashed through the windows of the school and danced along the walls, like a searchlight from a prison yard. The lone figure, dressed in faded Army fatigues, dove into the recessed entry of a classroom, pressed against the cool wall and hid from discovery. The light passed by, racing farther down the hall and finally disappearing into the night.

"I have located the enemy," the low, raspy voice whispered. "I have located the enemy, but she was able to escape."

The soldier punched the wall, then moved out of the classroom entrance and looked up and down the empty hall. With a stride reminiscent of marching, long legs carried the warrior back to the main entrance and to the darkened staircase that led to the basement. Combat-booted footsteps echoed off the walls of the stairwell as the camouflage on the fatigue disappeared into the darkness of the lower level. Finally, a click of a penlight created a small point of light, partially illuminating a face smeared with black face paint and shadows. Then the footsteps continued, combining with the sounds of the old school: water dripping from ancient pipes, wind whistling through broken windows, and the scurry of rodents finding a safer place to nest. At last, they stopped for a moment. The sound of rusted hinges rang through the basement, and the boots moved forward a few steps.

The narrow beam swept the wall and stopped at the framed photo hanging from a rusted nail stuck into the crumbling mortar in the brick. As the light grew closer, the photo became more visible. Although badly faded and stained by mold and humidity, the subject of the photo was apparent. Kristen Banks, in what looked to be her senior year high school photo, smiled at the beam of light.

"I only wanted to love you," the low voice whispered as a gloved hand delicately traced the edge of the face. "I only wanted to make you see that I was better for you than Danny. I only wanted a chance. And if you had lived, you would have given me that chance."

The glove fisted. "I deserved that chance," the whisper changed to a growl. "I deserved you. You didn't have to die. If you had only let me take you. You didn't have to die."

Pounding the wall next to the photo with both hands, the penlight slipped and clattered to the ground.

An anguished moan echoed in the confines of the small mechanical room. "I didn't kill you." It was more of a plea than a statement. "It was an accident. Just an accident."

Squatting down, the soldier reached for the penlight on the floor, but now its beam was focused on a lifeless body sprawled on the floor on the other side of the room. "But now it looks like I'm going to have to kill yet again."

Chapter Twenty-three

Bradley was standing in the driveway, waiting for her when she pulled up to the house. He was dressed in a t-shirt and sweatpants, but he looked every bit a knight on a white charger when he opened her door and pulled her into his arms. "Are you okay?" he breathed into her hair.

She felt the tension and fear fade as the strength of his love poured into her. She leaned against him, burying her face in his shoulder, breathing in his scent, and nodded. "I am now," she whispered. "Thank you."

She could feel him nod, but he just held her for a few more moments. Finally, his embrace lessened, and he leaned away from her to look into her eyes. "What happened?" he asked, his voice a little less soothing and a little more professional.

"I'll tell you as soon as we get inside," she said. "I really need to put my feet up; my legs are still a little shaky."

He wrapped his arms around her shoulders and walked her across the lawn, up the stairs and into the house, positioning himself so she was always shielded by his body. He started to walk her over to the couch, then stopped and looked down at her. "Bathroom?" he asked.

A genuine smile appeared on her slightly pale face. "Yes," she said. "That would be essential."

He leaned down and kissed her forehead. "I'll make you some tea," he replied, releasing her. "Then you can sit down and tell me all about it."

"Thanks," she replied, walking to the downstairs powder room.

When she walked back into the kitchen, she saw the kettle was on the stove, a cup with a tea bag on the counter, and a plate of cookies was next to it. She sighed softly. *What a wonderful man.*

She turned the corner to walk into the living room and realized that Andrew had arrived and was waiting nervously next to the front door. Mary walked into the room and made her way over to Bradley, who was building a fire in the fireplace.

"I know it's not that cold," he said. "But I thought it would be comforting."

Nodding, she placed her hand on his shoulder. "Bradley, I want to introduce you to my client, Andrew Tyler," she said.

Bradley looked up at Mary and then followed the direction of her gaze. "Hi, Andrew," Bradley said, standing up. "Nice to meet you."

"Mary, I'm so sorry I left you," Andrew stammered. "Suddenly I was so afraid. I don't know what came over me."

"That's okay, Andrew," she said. "Kristen helped me get away."

"Get away?" Bradley asked. "What the hell happened tonight? And what's the recent murder you were talking about?"

Mary turned to Bradley and scarcely shook her head, glancing in Andrew's direction.

"He doesn't…" Bradley began.

"No," Mary replied. "He doesn't."

She turned back to Andrew. "Why don't you come in," she said. "And we can talk about what I discovered tonight and a few other things. I want Bradley to be part of this because he's the Chief of Police in Freeport, and I thought he would be able to help us."

Andrew entered the room and sat down on a chair across from the couch. Just then the kettle whistled, and Bradley left the room to pour the tea. Mary strolled over to the couch and sat down.

"I'm just horrified by my behavior," Andrew said, sitting forward in the chair and clasping his hands together. "I've never done anything like that before."

121

"Well, it was a pretty tense situation," Mary said. "And I suppose part of the error was mine. I didn't ask you all of the questions I should have when we first started to work together."

Andrew sat back in the chair. "Ask away," he said. "I am an open book."

Bradley sat down next to Mary on the couch and placed her tea on the coffee table in front of them. "Thank you," she said to Bradley, clasping his hand in hers. "I was just going to ask Andrew some questions."

"Yeah, that's a good idea," Bradley replied. "Because I really want to start hearing some answers."

"Andrew, you mentioned to me that you read about me in the paper," she said. "Do you get the paper every day?"

He nodded. "Yeah, I subscribe," he said. "It's pretty much the first thing I do every morning. I get my coffee and read my paper."

"Do you remember what was in today's paper?" she asked.

He started to speak, then stopped, and a puzzled look came over his face. "Huh, that's funny," he said. "No, I don't. But, you know, it was a pretty stressful day."

She smiled encouragingly. "And when was the last time you went to work?" she questioned him.

"Just yester…" he began, then stopped. "No, I didn't go yesterday." He thought about it for a few moments, looking down at the floor. He looked up, confused. "Why can't I remember when I last went to work?"

"Perhaps the best thing to do is remember the last thing you did," Mary suggested, "and we can go from there."

Andrew nodded, leaned forward and placed his elbows on his knees and his chin on his hands. "Okay, I remember going through my recycling bin to find the paper with the article about you in it," he glanced up at her with chagrin. "Sorry, I threw you away at first."

"No problem," Mary replied. "But that tells me that was about a week or so ago, because I was several layers down in the recycling bin."

"Yeah. Yeah, I think it was like Monday or Tuesday of last week. So, I reread it and decided that I was going to call you first thing in the morning," he said. "Because I'd pretty much run out of ideas to solve Miss Banks' murder."

"What time of that day was that?" Bradley asked.

"It was early evening," Andrew replied. "Because I'd spent the day at work, and I was going to go back to the school that night."

"Did you go to the school?" Mary asked.

Andrew nodded slowly. "Yes. I went to the school," he said, his voice halting. "And I noticed that there had been some vandalism, which isn't a surprise because it's an old, abandoned building."

"What kind of vandalism?" Bradley asked.

"The window in the entrance door had been broken," he said.

"So someone had access to the interior of the school?" Mary verified.

"Yeah, but the kids won't go in there because they think it's haunted," he replied with a smile.

"When I went to meet you, the window wasn't broken," Mary said.

Andrew shrugged. "I guess I must have fixed it."

"What happened next?" Bradley encouraged.

"I went inside the school," Andrew replied, and then he thought about it for a moment. "I heard something. I heard something down in the basement."

He sat up and looked off into the distance. "I went downstairs," he continued slowly. "I was worried that someone would get hurt down there."

"And then what happened?" Mary asked softly.

Andrew's eyes widened, and his jaw dropped. He looked down at himself and then up at Mary and Bradley. "I never came back up," he whispered hoarsely. "I never came back up those stairs."

He looked to Mary for verification, and she slowly nodded. "You never did," she said. "Someone murdered you down in the basement of the school last week. And I don't think your murder has been discovered yet."

"Someone murdered me?" he choked. "Why would someone murder me?"

"Because you were getting too close to solving the murder of Kristen Banks," Bradley suggested. "And they needed to cover their tracks."

He buried his face in his hands. "I'm dead," he cried. "I'm really dead." Then he lifted his head and stared at Mary. "And that guy... the one who killed me...he was there tonight. He was going to try and kill you," he exclaimed. "Oh, Mary, I'm so sorry. You could have died."

Chapter Twenty-four

"Yes," Bradley said, looking down at Mary, his face deadly serious. "You could have. And I don't understand why you would put yourself in that kind of situation."

"I didn't realize how recently Andrew had died," Mary explained. "I thought he'd been dead awhile and his teacher's death was what kept him from moving on."

Andrew stared at her. "You knew I was dead when you first met me?" he asked.

"Well, your slit wrists kind of gave it away," she said.

Shocked, Andrew stared down at his wrists. "I never noticed them. It looks like I killed myself," he said, and then he added angrily, "I didn't kill myself. I wouldn't have killed myself." He looked up at Mary. "Why didn't you tell me?"

"Because you were so focused on your teacher, I thought it would be better to get the crime solved first. Then you could deal with the reality of your death," she said. "But I thought since the case was forty years old, there wasn't a lot of risk involved. And I have to confess that I thought you'd become despondent and had taken your own life."

"Why do you believe me now?" he asked.

Mary took a deep breath. "Tonight, when we were searching the desk, you told me you that you'd read the article about me," she said. "And since the article has only been out for a couple of weeks, I suddenly realized that you hadn't been dead for very long. And you certainly didn't act despondent when we were searching for the secret panel. You were excited and eager to learn more. That's when I realized I'd made a terrible mistake."

"And that's when we heard the noise," Andrew added.

"The noise?" Bradley asked. "Are you telling me that the killer was in the school with you tonight?"

Mary looked up and met Bradley's eyes. "Yes, I think he was," she said. "I grabbed the drawer, and I was going to try and get out before he caught me."

Bradley's jaw tightened. "You were going to try and outrun a killer?" he asked. "And you didn't think to call me?"

"There wasn't time," she said. "Even with your sirens blazing, it would have taken you at least twenty minutes."

"And you couldn't have called the local police?" Bradley asked.

"I thought about it," she said. "But then I realized two things. One, that I was in a building that also held a murdered body that no one had found yet. And two, I didn't know who the killer was. He could be a cop."

"Wait," Andrew interrupted. "Are you sure my body's in the school?"

She nodded. "Every time I've met you at the school, you've come from the inside to let me in," she said. "This time, I peeked through the window and saw you come up from the basement. It makes sense that the killer left you down there."

"Let's go back to you being trapped in an abandoned building with a killer," Bradley said. "I'm not quite over that yet."

Mary nodded. "Kristen opened the secret panel in the drawer and gave me the journal and all of her letters," she said. "Then she took the drawer and walked to the stairway on the other side of the school. She threw the drawer down the stairs and caused enough noise to draw the killer to her. He ran past the classroom—"

"Stop," Bradley said, his voice tight with emotion. "You heard the killer run past the classroom you were hiding in? He was that close?"

"Yes, he was," she said. "Then Kristen made even more noise, and he ran past the classroom and down the hall. As soon as I thought he was far enough away, I ran out of the classroom, down the stairs and out to the parking lot."

Bradley shook his head, rose from the couch and then walked away from Mary, into the kitchen.

"Mary, I'm so sorry," Andrew said. "I didn't realize how dangerous this was going to be."

"No, it's not your fault, Andrew," she said. "I should have realized. I should have taken precautions. I'm the one who acted like an amateur."

"Are you going to give up on the case?" he asked.

She shook her head. "No, I won't give up on the case," she said. "But I have a feeling I'm going to have a new partner."

"Damn right," Bradley called from the other room.

Andrew looked from Mary to Bradley and shook his head. "I think I'd better go now," he said. "I'll see you tomorrow."

"Okay," Mary said. "See you tomorrow, Andrew."

Mary watched him fade away, and then, once he was gone, she took a deep breath. Standing up, she walked to the kitchen where Bradley stood staring out the back window, his hands clutching the counter next to the sink. Biting her lower lip, she watched him for a moment. Every muscle was taut, and his breathing was slow and deliberate.

Stepping forward, she slipped her arms around his waist and laid her head against his back. "I'm so sorry," she whispered. "I was stupid and careless. Please forgive me."

She felt his quick intake of breath, felt the expansion of his chest and the slow, shuddering release of air. "Mary," he said, his voice hoarse. "You could have…"

He turned around and pulled her into his arms, crushing her against him, as he held her tightly. He didn't say a word, he just held her and she could feel the erratic thumping of his heart against his chest. "I'm so sorry," she whispered again. "I'm so sorry."

Finally, his muscles relaxed and he leaned away from her, still holding her in his arms. "I'm as mad as hell at you," he said softly.

"You should be," she agreed.

"Never again," he stated. "Never again will you put yourself in a situation that could endanger your life."

She nodded mutely.

"Damn it," he said, shaking his head. "Losing you would kill me. The thought of losing you has nearly killed me. I'm not going to be logical. I'm not going to be fair. No more, Mary. No more."

Chapter Twenty-five

Mary sat in the corner of the couch, sipping on her tea, hoping that the chamomile would work its magic and calm her still fluttering heart. She had lain in bed for an hour trying to quiet her mind long enough to fall asleep, but sleep was just not happening. Finally, she had given up and quietly padded downstairs to see if a cup of tea would help.

"Hey, how are you doing, champ?" Mike asked as he appeared next her on the other end of the couch.

She sighed and shook her head. "Well, no demons are coming after me," she said, staring at her cup. "So I guess I'm good."

"Yeah, well, we called in reinforcements, so you ought to be demon free for a while," he said. "But this has nothing to do with what you're feeling right now."

"I totally blew it this time," she said, and then she met his eyes. "By the way, thank you for warning me."

He shrugged. "It's all in the job description," he said softly. "But you really shouldn't be so hard on yourself."

"I should have asked Andrew some more questions," she argued. "I should have found out more about him."

"You had a man who still carried a spelling paper from his fourth grade teacher come to you for help," he said. "You were kind, and you were resourceful. And, yeah, you probably took a little more risk than you should have."

Mary put her cup down and laced her fingers over her belly. "I lot more risk," she said. "I keep forgetting that I'm pregnant."

He lifted an eyebrow skeptically, and she chuckled. "Okay, I don't forget," she admitted. "But when I think about what I can do, like dashing up stairs, I forget that I'm carrying a little person along with me and that's going to slow me down. And, I forget that I'm risking for two, not just one. I scared Bradley to death."

He stared at her for a long moment. "Do you think that Bradley's reaction would have been any less…" he searched for a word and then smiled at her, "volatile, if you had not been pregnant?"

"Well…" she began.

"You do!" he interrupted. "You think that he was scared to death for you because you're pregnant."

133

"Well I am a trained law enforcement professional," she argued.

"Who Bradley adores," he returned softly. "And who he worries about constantly."

She sat up in the couch. "What? He worries?"

Mike rolled his eyes. "Not just about your work," he said. "Although he does worry about that. But he worries that you're not getting enough sleep, you're not eating properly, you're not getting enough down time, you're not laughing as much as you used to or several dozen more things that flash through his mind throughout the day."

"Why?" Mary asked.

"Because he feels that when you agreed to marry him, you didn't agree to the package deal," he replied. "Suddenly you're not just married, you're a mom and you're going through your first pregnancy while you are taking on the responsibilities that a young wife shouldn't have to take on. You didn't really get a honeymoon stage; you just got blasted with the cold reality of life."

"But I like the cold reality of life," she argued and then she shook her head. "I mean, it's not a cold reality. I love my life."

"Do you?" Mike asked. "Do you really love it? And don't just answer 'yes' because it's the proper thing to do. It's just you and me, kid. Do you really love your life?"

Mary picked up her cup again, took a sip and thought about her answer. She thought about restless nights, padding back and forth to the bathroom instead of sleeping, aching body parts, upset stomachs and stretch marks. She thought about dirty dishes, dusty shelves and unfolded laundry. She thought about saving money, minivans instead of Roadsters, and flats instead of heels.

She took another sip of tea and then the little person inside of her moved. That was all it took for her to know her answer. Looking up at Mike, tears shining in her eyes, she smiled and nodded. "Yeah, I really love my life."

"I thought so," he replied. "But sometimes it's a good idea to do inventory and make sure."

She wiped away one stray tear and nodded. "So, how can I make sure Bradley knows I love this life?"

"Get enough sleep, eat properly, allow yourself some down time and laugh, a lot," he replied.

She grinned. "Does dark chocolate ice cream count as eating properly?" she asked.

He nodded. "Hey, it's dairy, right?"

"Right," she replied. "Thank you, Mike. You're the best friend I ever had."

He smiled at her. "Same here, kid," he replied as he slowly faded away. "Same here."

She placed her cup on the kitchen counter and walked upstairs to her bedroom. Standing next to the bed, she studied Bradley for a few moments. Even in sleep, his face seemed tense tonight and she knew she was the cause. She tried to climb into bed carefully, so as not to wake him, but failed miserably.

"Mary?" Bradley asked, his voice laced with sleep. "Are you okay?"

"Yes," she whispered. "I'm just coming back to bed. Go to sleep."

"Are you sure you're okay?" he asked again. This time his voice sounded more awake.

She leaned over and kissed him. "I'm fine," she said. "Just tired. Goodnight."

He lay quietly on the bed, feigning sleep, and waited for several minutes until he heard the soft, rhythmic sound of her breathing as she slept. Cautiously slipping out of the bed, he unknowingly imitated her earlier position and stood by the bed, watching her sleep. With a long, silent sigh, he shook his head. "Dammit Mary, I'm so sorry," he whispered harshly and then left the room.

An hour later Mike reappeared, his attention drawn by a sound coming from the basement. Gliding down the stairs, he found Bradley, wearing only pajama bottoms and bare feet, skipping back and forth in front of a punching bag that was hanging from a rafter in the basement. He was wearing boxing gloves and beating the leather sides with hard, even hits.

"Are you okay?" Mike asked him.

Ever since Mike had fooled Bradley into believing he could see ghosts, Bradley had been able to see Mike. Taking another couple more jabs at the bag, Bradley leaned forward, grabbed the bag to stop its movement and then looked over at Mike and shrugged. Mike leaned against a nearby pillar and folded his arms over his chest. "So, I'm taking that to mean no, you are not okay," he stated.

Sweat glistening on his chest, Bradley turned to him and shook his head. "No, actually, I'm not okay," he said. "So I came down here to be alone. You know alone." he added pointedly. "And beat something up."

"Yeah, alone sounds good. And I can fade out of here," he said. "But if you wouldn't mind, I just have one question. Why are you not fine?"

Bradley stepped away from the bag and looked at Mike. "I've screwed everything up," he

137

said. "I have totally, completely screwed everything up."

"Wow," Mike replied. "I hadn't realized that. But just to be sure I understand, what exactly are we talking about here?"

Bradley punched against the bag. "First of all," he said, his jaw tight, "I have totally ruined Mary's life."

Mike nodded. "Yeah, I can see that," he said.

"You can?" Bradley asked, turning suddenly towards Mike so the swinging bag hit him and made him stumble.

"Oh, yeah," Mike agreed, standing up, walking closer and meeting Bradley's eyes. "First of all, you force her to fall in love with you. She could have had her choice of guys, but no, you had to ruin things and be the only man she could spend her life with."

"Well," Bradley began, but Mike held his hand up, stopping him.

"Then, you give her a daughter, who she totally adores, especially when she thought she would never have the chance to have a baby," he said. "A daughter whose birth she experienced. A daughter she cared for so much, even before she met her, that she would not let Ian wipe out through hypnosis the traumatic things she experienced, because she always wanted to remember giving birth to Clarissa."

Bradley's eyes widened. "I didn't know—" he began, but Mike cut him off again.

"And then, you had the audacity to get her pregnant," Mike continued. "A dream she'd always had, but had almost given up on. And along with the morning sickness, the fatigue and the change in her size, she gets to participate in a miracle. She gets to feel a tiny person inside of her. She gets to know that she is a partner with God in the giving of life."

Mike shook his head. "Yeah, you suck, man," he said. "Big time."

Bradley pulled the gloves off his hands and then bent over and laid them down on the floor under the bag. He stood up and looked at Mike. "Once again," he said, his voice filled with emotion, "I owe you. Thank you."

Mike nodded and smiled. "Go upstairs to your wife," he said. "Stop worrying, and start enjoying the time you have together. You never know how much time you have on this earth with the people you love."

Bradley's eyes widened in concern. "Is that a warning?" he asked.

Shaking his head sadly, Mike started to fade away. "No, it's the voice of experience."

Chapter Twenty-six

"Hi, Mom," Mary said into the phone the next morning. She leaned back in her chair and propped her feet up on the desk. "Do you have a few minutes?"

Margaret O'Reilly strolled into her living room and sat on the couch, propping her feet up on the coffee table and unknowingly mimicking her daughter's position. "Of course," she replied. "I was looked for an excuse to not clean the refrigerator, and you've presented me with a fine one. How are you, darling?"

Suddenly all of the pent up emotions from the past few days escaped, and Mary's voice trembled. "Mom, I've had a really bad week so far," she cried.

"Oh, darling," Margaret said, sitting up in the couch. "What happened?"

Mary thought about telling her mother about the close call she'd experienced the night before and decided against it. There were some things Mary just didn't tell her mom, because she knew her mother would worry about her even more than she already did. Mary took a deep breath and went to the heart of what was really bothering here. "I don't think Kate and Rosie are my friends anymore," she said.

Margaret smiled to herself and shook her head. She had been in contact with both Rosie and Kate for the past few weeks, helping to plan the shower. She should have known her intuitive daughter would feel that they were keeping something from her. "Why do you think that?" she asked.

"They went shopping together, and they didn't even ask me?" she replied. "And then, when I found them there together, they lied to me."

"That must have made you feel sad," her mother sympathized.

"Yes. And a little angry," Mary admitted.

"Well, of course," Margaret empathized. "Who wouldn't be angry to discover her two best friends out shopping together? Unless…" She paused for a moment, letting the word hang. "No, never mind."

"Never mind what?" Mary asked, wiping a tear from her cheek.

"Well, the only time I didn't invite you to come shopping with me was when I was going Christmas shopping or birthday shopping for you," Margaret suggested. "But, really, Christmas is about two months away. That doesn't make sense."

"Oh, what if they were getting something for the baby?" Mary asked, a hint of relief in her voice.

"What if there were buying a gift together, and they didn't want me to see it?"

Margaret grinned and sat back on the couch again. "Would they do something like that?" she asked.

Mary exhaled and smiled. "Of course, that makes perfect sense now," she said. "How silly of me to be worried."

"Well, it's only natural for you to respond that way," her mother replied.

"Only natural if you're not thinking straight, and your hormones are crazy," Mary chuckled.

Her mother laughed softly. "Well, that's just another one of those maternity bonuses," she said. "So, how is everything else going?"

"Everyone is so excited about Friday night," Mary said. "It's so wonderful of all of you to drive up here to celebrate Halloween with us."

"Oh, now, we wouldn't miss it," Margaret said. "Your father and I plan on coming up early to help you take Clarissa trick-or-treating. We haven't done that in too many years."

"Clarissa will love that," Mary said. "She's been busy trying to find a ghost story to tell. She's even asked Maggie to help her find a real ghost."

"Ah, she's a bright girl," Margaret said. "And a determined one, too. I'll be surprised if she doesn't have the best story of the night. And how is Bradley coming along with his story?"

Mary chuckled. "Well, he's certainly practicing," she said. "And I'm sure by Friday night he'll be just fine."

"He's a good man," Margaret said. "Playing along with our family's strange traditions."

"I actually think he's looking forward to it," Mary said. "And he even volunteered to take care of the refreshments, knowing how tired I've been lately. That is so unlike Bradley. He usually hates doing things like this."

Margaret grinned, knowing that she, Rosie and Kate had told Bradley several weeks ago that they were going to take care of all the food for the shower. "Well, good for him," Margaret agreed. "And I'm sure it will be delicious."

"It might be pizza," Mary warned.

"If I don't have to cook or clean up, it's a treat no matter what it is," her mother replied. "And how are you feeling?"

"Good," she said. "Actually, much better now that I've spoken with you. You seem to know how to say all the right things. Thanks, Mom."

"Well, thank you for taking the time to call," her mother replied. "I always love hearing from you."

Mary sighed. "Well, I should get back to work," she said. "I love you, Mom. I can't wait to see you."

"I love you too, Mary-Mary," her mother replied. "You make sure you don't work too hard. And be sure to drink plenty of water and eat sensibly."

"I was actually thinking about walking across to the bakery and buying a brownie for a snack," Mary confessed.

"And would it have nuts in it?" Margaret asked.

"Yes," Mary replied.

"Then that's a protein," Margaret answered. "That sounds very sensible if you ask me. And, if they happen to have freshly baked ones on Friday, I wouldn't mind being sensible with you."

Laughing, Mary nodded. "That's a deal, Mom," she said.

Chapter Twenty-seven

"Okay, I'm going to pull the cruiser back behind the school in the alley," Bradley said when they were about a block away from the school, "so we're not too noticeable. I called a friend from the local police force, and he's going to meet us here in a few minutes."

"I'd like to get out first," Mary said. "We might attract the killer if I'm out there alone."

Bradley pulled over to the curb and turned to his wife. "You do realize that every single molecule in my body is screaming to keep you in the car where you will be safe?" he asked.

She leaned across the seat and kissed him. "Yes, I know," she said, taking his hands in hers. "The door I will be standing in front of is shielded on both sides by an overhang, so a sniper would not be able to get to me from there. And there is half a city block worth of parking lot between the entrance and the street. So, it would be nearly impossible for someone to shoot at me from there. And, I will only be alone for less than three minutes." She met his eyes. "But, if you ask me not to go out there and do my job, I'll stay."

He closed his eyes and sighed deeply. "Three minutes," he said, looking at her and then putting the car back in gear. "And then I'm at your side."

"Perfect," she said with a smile.

The sun was shining down on the cracked, concrete parking lot, and the temperature was in the mid-60s. Mary wrapped her wool cardigan around herself and hurriedly walked to the front entrance. She peered through the door to try and catch a glimpse of Andrew as he came upstairs, hoping to get a better idea of where he came from.

"Is there something I can help you with?"

Mary nearly squealed when the deep voice rang out from behind her. She turned to see an older man standing at the edge of the portico, his hands shoved inside the bomber jacket he was wearing. *He could be carrying a gun,* she thought. *Dammit!*

"Oh, I'm just waiting for someone," she replied with a friendly shrug. "But thanks for asking."

He shifted his hands in his pocket and stepped forward. "Who are you waiting for?"

"Me," Bradley said, stepping up behind the man and towering over him, the badge on his chest glinting in the morning sun. "Does that answer your question, Mister…"

"Howse. Mitchell Howse," the man replied, pulling his hand slowly from his jacket.

Mary jumped forward, positioning herself between Bradley and Mitchell. "Oh, I'm sorry," she said sweetly. "Leg cramp. They happen all the time."

Mitchell stuck his hand back in his pocket. "So, if you don't mind me asking, what are you doing here?"

"Well, actually, I do mind," Bradley said, taking Mary's arm and gently guiding her behind him. "But, if you don't mind, I'd like to ask you a couple of questions."

Rolling back on his heels, Mitchell shook his head. "I'm guessing you don't have any jurisdiction here in Polo," he replied.

Bradley shook his head. "No, you're right, I don't," he said. "But I figured you wouldn't mind answering some questions, just between friends."

Mitchell took a step back, away from them, and shook his head. "I guess I just don't feel all that friendly towards you."

He turned around and slowly walked away from them. When he got about halfway across the parking lot, a Polo Police Department cruiser pulled in and came alongside him. The driver rolled his window down and chatted with Mitchell for a few minutes, and then Mitchell stepped away from the car, waved at the officer and continued on his way.

The car pulled up next to the portico, and a police officer about Bradley's age stepped out. "Hey, Alden, good to see you," the officer said.

Bradley stepped forward and shook the officer's hand. "Hey, Kris, thanks for meeting us here," he said. "Let me introduce my wife, Mary."

Kris walked over to Mary and took her hand. "Hi, it's good to meet you," he said.

"Thanks," Mary said. "I appreciate you coming out and meeting us. Can I just ask, before we go any further, do you know the man you just spoke with?"

Kris automatically looked over his shoulder and then back at Mary. "Oh, Mitch? Yeah, I know him," he said. "This is a pretty small town, so we all know each other. Why?"

"Oh, I just wondered about him," she replied.

"Well, Mitch has his own construction business," Kris said. "He never married once he got back from Vietnam. I heard he'd been sweet on someone here in town, but nothing ever came of it. He's got a small circle of friends, mostly the folks he went to school with."

"Thanks," Mary said. "Do you think he could ever be violent?"

Kris looked back over his shoulder again and studied the man who was now about a block away from them. He shrugged. "Well, I guess just about anyone could be violent given the right motivation."

He turned back and looked at Bradley. "So, what is this all about?" he asked.

"My wife has a client who has recently turned up missing," Bradley explained.

"He was investigating the death of his fourth grade teacher," Mary explained.

Kris nodded. "Oh, yeah, I met that guy at the station," he said. "Andrew, right?"

Mary nodded. "Yes, Andrew Tyler," Mary said. "He was supposed to meet with me several days ago, and he never showed up. I've been trying to get hold of him, but nothing's working. He was checking out the school for clues, and I'm worried that something might have happened to him."

"So, you think he might be here?" Kris asked.

Mary shrugged. "Well, it's the first place I considered," she said. "And I was hoping we could check it out."

Kris walked over to the door and tugged. "Sorry, it's locked," he said. "And we don't have a key. And I really can't justify breaking down the door unless there's a missing person's report."

Mary slipped between Kris and the door. Andrew was on the other side and he unlocked the door for her. She pulled it open and turned to Kris. "Well, look at that," she said. "It just opened for me."

Kris looked at Mary and then looked at the door. "Well, that was spooky."

Bradley shook his head. "You have no idea."

Chapter Twenty-eight

"Can we go to the library again today?" Clarissa asked Maggie at lunch. "I'd like to see your friend again. He was real nice."

With a mouthful of her sandwich, Maggie nodded. "Sure," she murmured, chewing a couple more times and then swallowing. "But is he gonna be scary enough for the ghost story time?"

Clarissa took a bite of her own sandwich, chewing slowly while she pondered Maggie's words. Finally she looked up and shrugged. "I guess just talking to a ghost and seeing books float is pretty scary," she reasoned. "And I really don't know if I want to see a gross ghost."

Maggie nodded. "Gross ghosts are pretty creepy," she agreed. "And they make you have nightmares."

Clarissa picked up a mini carrot and stuck it into her ranch dip, but just before eating it, she turned to her friend. "Do you see many gross ghosts?" she asked.

"Not lately," she said, helping herself to one of Clarissa's carrots and some dip. "But before Mary moved in, I had lots of them."

"Why? What happened when my mom moved in?" Clarissa asked.

Maggie reached in her lunchbox and pulled out a bag of chips. She ripped the bag open and placed it directly between them. "It was like she had a stronger pull," Maggie said. "So instead of coming to my house when they had a problem, they went to your house."

"Do you think lots of gross ghosts come to my house every day?" Clarissa asked as she helped herself to the chips.

"I don't know," Maggie said. "Do you think Mary would tell you?"

Clarissa shook her head. "Probably not," she said. "She wouldn't want me to worry."

"Would you? Worry?"

"Can you worry about something you don't see?" Clarissa asked her friend.

Maggie shrugged as she dunked a chip into the ranch dip. "I don't know. A lot of people do it," she said. "My mom says those people are borrowing trouble."

"That's a weird thing to say," Clarissa said. "Why are grownups so weird?"

Sighing, Maggie took a final bite of her sandwich. "I don't know," she said. "Maybe that's one of the things that happen when you get puberty."

"Oh, that makes sense," Clarissa agreed. She put the lid on the ranch dip and placed the plastic container back in her lunchbox. "Do you think we're still going to be friends when we're grown up?"

"Of course," Maggie said, packing up her own things. "We're the 'doption girls. We have to stay together."

"That's right," Clarissa agreed with a wide smile. "We'll be friends forever."

The climbed down from the lunch table and walked to the door to go outside for recess. "Just two more days until Halloween," Clarissa said as they passed the poster for the Halloween parade that was posted on the door. "I can't wait."

"Me, too," Maggie agreed. "Is your mom going to tell ghost stories to our class?"

Clarissa shook her head. "No, she doesn't want everyone to think our family is weird. So, she's just gonna act like a normal mom and pass out candy and treats and stuff."

"Yeah, my mom said I shouldn't tell ghost stories either," Maggie added. "She said people don't always understand stuff like that."

"I don't get why people don't believe in ghosts," Clarissa said with a sigh. "I mean, they are all around us."

"People are just weird," Maggie said.

Chapter Twenty-nine

"Okay, we're not going to do any weird stuff here," Kris Dore stated as they walked into the school. "I read that article about you. You're like some psychic investigator, right?"

"Well, not quite," Mary replied.

"See, that's what I told my wife," he interrupted. "That stuff's not real. The paper made all that crap up. You should really see about suing them. That's what I'd do; sue the pants off of them."

"Well, actually…" Mary tried again.

"No, you don't have to explain it to me," he said. "I know how unreasonable these reporters can be. I can't tell you how many times my words have been taken out of context and reported in the paper. Sure, maybe I said them, but I didn't mean them to come out like that."

Mary glanced past Kris to Bradley, who grinned and shrugged at her. "I thought we should check the basement," Mary suggested when Kris started to lead them to the staircase.

"Yeah, but I thought the fourth grade teacher died upstairs," he said. "Wouldn't he be upstairs?"

"He mentioned something about checking out the basement the last time we spoke," Mary said. "So, I really think we should try there first."

Kris shrugged. "Okay, you're the psychic," he said facetiously, laughing at his own joke.

"Yeah," Mary replied with a forced laugh. "I guess I am."

At the top of the staircase to the basement, Kris put his arm out to stop Mary from venturing down, and then he turned to Bradley. "Are you sure you want your little lady to go downstairs?" he asked. "I mean, if we do find a body, it could be a little ugly down there."

Seeing the look of astonished outrage on Mary's face, Bradley bit back his laughter. He met her eyes and shook his head, sending her a subtle warning. In his heart, he really wanted Mary to put Kris in his place, but they needed his help to find Andrew. "No, that's okay, Kris," Bradley replied. "I think Mary can handle it."

Kris dropped his arm. "Okay, you're the boss," he said, and with his flashlight beaming, he led the way down the stairs.

"Um, we could use the lights," Mary commented before she stepped down the shadowed stairs.

"I'm sorry, what sweetheart?" Kris asked.

157

Mary reached over and flipped the switch that illuminated the lights over the staircase. "The lights work," she said.

"You knew that because you're psychic, right?" he laughed again.

Bradley stepped up next to Mary. "Don't say anything you'll regret later," he whispered.

She sighed and nodded. "That must be it," she called down the stairs, forcing her laughter once again.

Once they all reached the basement, Mary looked around and saw Andrew standing next to a small door that looked like it led to a utility room. She was getting hungry, and once again, she really needed to use the bathroom. Not wanting to take the time to let Kris discover the body, which, she mused, could take days, she pointed to the utility room and said, "Why don't we check that room."

"Yeah, he's probably not in there," Kris said, moving in the other direction. "That's a utility room, and it's probably locked."

Mary sent a wordless plea for help to Bradley, who quickly walked over to that room and turned the handle. "Nope, it's open," he called. "But you should probably be the first one inside, because it's your jurisdiction."

Shaking his head, Kris walked back to the room. "It's nice of you to appease the little lady and all," Kris said. "But really, she should leave the investigations to trained professionals."

"Actually, Mary is—" Bradley began.

"Very grateful you'd check this out first," she said. "And after this, we can go wherever you think."

Kris pushed the door open with an audible sigh. "Fine," he said.

He whipped his flashlight beam across the floor in a cursory manner, not expecting anything, and nearly dropped it when he found the body in the corner of the room. "Well, I'll be damned," he said. "There's a body in here."

Mary closed her eyes for a brief moment and prayed for strength. "Oh, wow, how amazing," she said, trying hard not to sound sarcastic. "Is he still alive?"

Kris started walking into the room, his flashlight focused on the body, when Mary leaned in and turned on the light. He turned to her in surprise.

"Crime scene," she said, waving the piece of cloth she used to protect any fingerprints on the switch. "I didn't want you to inadvertently step on any evidence or disturb a blood trail."

He shook his head. "Oh, yeah, you're right," he stuttered.

Mary studied him. His eyes were wide, and his face was pale. "Have you ever seen a dead body before?" she asked.

"No," he said, his body beginning to sway. "And I think I might be getting…"

Bradley grabbed him and pulled him out of the room, dragging him to a wastepaper basket in the corner of the room where he emptied out the contents of his stomach. "You'll feel much better once you get that out of your system," Bradley said.

Kris retched again, and Bradley shook his head. "Dude, you really need to lay off those donuts."

Chapter Thirty

"Well, apple cider donuts are always delicious," Rosie said, flipping through a cookbook. "Although, perhaps we should be thinking about a cake."

Kate looked up from her list and sighed. "There are so many options," she said. "And I know we want everything to be perfect. What do you think, Margaret?"

Margaret O'Reilly's image was on the screen of the electronic tablet that was propped up in the middle of Rosie's kitchen table. "I think apple cider donuts sound delicious," Margaret said. "And since it's Halloween night, they seem appropriate. Or, we could do something with pumpkin."

"Pumpkin cheesecake," Rosie exclaimed, hurriedly turning the pages in the book. "I have the most amazing recipe for it."

"Oh, that does sound good," Margaret said. "What if we do one cheesecake of pumpkin and another of salted caramel? I have a lovely recipe for that kind."

Kate leaned back in her chair. "Well, if we're going to do those two, we also have to have a dark chocolate one," she insisted.

"Yes. Yes, we do," Margaret agreed with a chuckle. "It wouldn't be a balanced meal without chocolate."

All three women laughed, and Kate jotted down the three desserts. "Okay, I have the recipe for that one, so each of us will bring a cheesecake," Kate said, and then she turned to Rosie. "But, I've never made a cheesecake before, so can I come over here and make it with you watching over my shoulder?"

"Of course, dear," Rosie said. "And I'm sure your cheesecake will be delicious."

"Thank you, Rosie," Kate replied, and then she looked down at her list. "Great. I think we have the menu. Is there anything else we have to discuss?"

"I hesitate to bring this up," Margaret said. "But I think you need to know. Mary called me this morning, and she was upset."

"Goodness, why?" Rosie asked. "Is there something wrong with the baby?"

"No, nothing like that," Margaret reassured her. "She was upset because she discovered you two shopping together and she hadn't been invited."

"I knew she didn't believe us," Rosie said. "It was the purses in the child seat, wasn't it?"

162

"Well, she didn't go into that much detail," Margaret replied. "But she did know that you weren't telling her the truth."

"That's what you get for trying to lie to a private investigator," Kate said with a sigh. "So, is she still pretty upset?"

"No, I don't think so," Margaret answered. "I suggested that perhaps the two of you were shopping for a baby gift for her and that's why you didn't want her around."

"Oh, that was brilliant," Rosie said. "And when she finds out what we were really doing, she's going to be so surprised!"

"Speaking of surprises," Kate said, "Margaret, when are you and your family arriving?"

"I told Mary that Timothy and I would be coming early enough to help her take Clarissa trick-or-treating," Margaret said. "But he has the entire day off, so if you need us to come even earlier, that would be easy. The boys will come closer to the event."

"I know that Mary's working on a case right now," Kate said. "And she's signed up for the Halloween party at Clarissa and Maggie's class. So, I don't think she'll be hanging around her house too much."

"Stanley volunteered to keep her busy and away from things if we need him to," Rosie added.

"And since Bradley *volunteered* to make all the food for the family get-together," Margaret said with a chuckle, "perhaps we could have him barricade the dining room and kitchen so Mary can't see inside and tell her it's because he wants to surprise her."

"Oh, that's a great idea," Kate agreed. "Especially since Bradley is working so hard to make the refreshments."

Rosie looked from Kate to Margaret and shook her head. "But I thought we were making the refreshments."

"We are, darling," Margaret said. "But Bradley is pretending to do it so Mary doesn't get suspicious."

"Oh," Rosie said. "Well, isn't that clever of him." She sighed contentedly. "I just adore clever people."

"I just want to say thank you to both of you," Margaret said. "It's so comforting to me to know that Mary is surrounded with good friends who love her and do so much for her."

"Well, we simply adore her," Rosie said. "She's done so much for us. I don't know what we would do if Mary wasn't in our lives."

Kate nodded. "I agree," she said. "She is a good woman, Margaret. You did a good job."

Margaret laughed. "Yes I did," she teased. "And I will take all the credit for how she turned out. Well, I suppose I should admit that she gets her fearlessness from Timothy. I'm a bit of a coward."

Chapter Thirty-one

"I'm not a coward," Kris insisted as he walked back into the utility room. "I just had a queasy stomach, that's all."

Mary smiled sympathetically. "I understand how that is," she said. "So, do you need to call the coroner?"

"No," he insisted walking over to the body. "I can examine the body myself."

He leaned over the sprawled body, bracing his hand on the wall so he wouldn't get too close, and slowly looked down. "Well," he finally said, turning to Mary and Bradley with a superior smile on his face. "I'd say we have a suicide on our hands. Seems like your client wasn't quite as rational as you thought him to be."

"A suicide?" Mary asked. "How did he die?"

Kris pointed in the direction of the body. "His wrists are slit," he said. "It's an obvious suicide."

Mary walked over to stand next to the body, being sure she didn't step too close and disturb the still sticky pools of blood. She slowly looked around the area and then turned back to Kris. "Where's the knife?" she asked.

"The knife?" he repeated.

She nodded her head. "The knife he needed to slit his own wrists," she said. "I don't see it."

Kris looked a little put out. "Well, he obviously dumped it," he said.

Mary nodded slowly. "So, he slit both of his wrists and then walked somewhere else in the basement, got rid of the knife and then came back here to die?"

"It could happen," Kris defended.

"It could," Mary agreed. "But then we would see a blood trail, wouldn't we?"

He looked at the body and then down at the floor. The blood was only pooled around the area where Andrew's body lay. "Well, maybe he cleaned it up," he suggested.

"Maybe," Bradley said slowly. "But, perhaps this was a murder that was meant to look like a suicide."

"Why would you jump to that conclusion?" Kris asked. "The guy was obviously a little unbalanced in the first place. He actually told me he thought he saw his teacher's ghost when he was still a kid. I mean, if that's not unbalanced, what is?"

Frustrated, Mary walked away from the crime scene and out the door into the basement. She found an old, metal folding chair and sat down, her temper nearing its boiling point.

"He thinks I killed myself, doesn't he?" Andrew asked, appearing next to her.

She nodded. "Yes," she sighed and then replied quietly. "But he's an ass, so don't pay any attention to him."

Andrew smiled half-heartedly. "He never liked me," he admitted.

"What?" Mary asked, turning to him. "Kris?"

"Yeah, he never liked me after I dumped his sister," Andrew admitted.

"Wait, he knows you?"

"Of course, it's a small town…" he began.

"And everyone knows everyone else," Mary finished. "But you dated his sister?"

"Yeah, a long time ago," he said. "Everyone thought we were going to get married, but, you know, it just didn't feel right. So, I moved to Chicago, started my own computer business, made a lot of money and then moved back to town."

"By a lot, you mean…" Mary asked.

Andrew sighed. "A lot," he said. "Enough to retire before I was fifty and buy an old school that no one wanted," he said. "I still dabble in investments, but I'm what you would call independently wealthy."

"Did his sister ever marry?" Mary asked.

"Yeah, she's got a bunch of kids, and they live on a farm outside of town," he replied. "I think she's real happy."

Mary took a deep breath and stood up.

"Where are you going?" Andrew asked.

"Well, I'm either going to prove a point, or I'm going to be considered a nutcase in this small town," she said, and then she turned to him. "Do you mind going back in where your body is laying?"

"Not if it will help them try and solve my murder and Miss Banks' murder, too," he replied.

She nodded. "Okay, come on, I'm going to need your help."

They walked back into the room where Bradley and Kris were arguing. "Why didn't you tell us that Andrew Tyler dated your sister?" Mary asked.

Kris' jaw dropped, and he stared at her. "What? Who told you that?"

"He dated her," Mary continued. "And everyone thought they were going to get married. But then he broke it off with her and moved to Chicago."

"Is that true, Kris?" Bradley asked.

"Did you call someone?" Kris asked.

"That's not the point," Mary said. "Is it true that you were already prejudiced against Andrew?"

"Ask him about the ticket he gave me on my first night back in town," Andrew coached.

"And how about the ticket you gave him on his first night back in town?" Mary asked.

"For jaywalking on a side street," Andrew added.

"For jaywalking on a side street?" Mary repeated incredulously.

"Are you bugged?" Kris asked, walking over and aggressively confronting Mary. "How could you know this?"

Bradley walked over and put his hand on Mary's shoulder. Mary smiled up at him, then turned to Kris and met his eyes. "Because Andrew is in this room right now," she said. "And he told me about what you did. He told me about your sister. And he told me he was murdered. And now, quite frankly, I'm wondering if you didn't have a hand in it because you have so much hate for him."

Kris stepped back and shook his head. "You're crazy," he said. "You're a nutcase. And I don't have to stand here and take this shit from you."

"Ask him if the police chief knows about the time he stole a car?" Andrew said.

"Well, before you leave, I have one more question," Mary said. "Does the police chief know about the stolen car?"

Kris froze in his tracks, and he slowly looked around the room.

"Tell him that Debbie told me all about that," Andrew added.

"Debbie told Andrew all about that," Mary said.

Kris' breathing intensified, and his eyes widened. "Where is he?" he asked, his voice shaking.

"He's standing right next to you," Mary said. "Can't you feel the hairs on the back of your neck standing up because you can feel his cold, dead breath on you?"

Kris grabbed the back of his neck and ran from the room. "I'm getting out of here."

"Um, Mary, I'm still standing right here, next to you," Andrew said.

Mary shrugged. "I was just practicing my dramatic storytelling skills," she replied softly. "Pretty good, huh?"

"Damn good," Bradley chuckled softly. "Come on, I think we can call the Ogle County Coroner now. I don't think Kris is going to argue with you at all."

"Thanks, Mary," Andrew said. "Now we just have to find out who did it."

Chapter Thirty-two

The library was busier when Kate brought Clarissa and Maggie there right after school. "Wow," Maggie said. "Where did all these people come from?"

Kate looked around and then saw a small flyer attached to a bulletin board. "Oh, there's a local writer here today, telling ghost stories," Kate said. "I remember hearing her tell stories years ago at the Stephenson County Historical Society, and she was pretty good. Would you like to listen?"

"Are they real stories?" Clarissa asked. "Can she really see ghosts?"

Kate paused for a moment and then shook her head. "No, I don't think so," she said. "Most of her stories are collected from other people who have seen ghosts."

"Well, we can try it for a little while," Maggie said. "But if she's boring, can we go look at other stuff?"

"And by other stuff, what do you mean?" Kate asked.

Maggie looked around the large room. "Well, it's pretty crowded down here," she said. "And upstairs is pretty boring. Could we go outside to the statue?"

"If you are going to do that, you need to tell me first," Kate said. "And then you can go."

"Thanks, Mom," Maggie said. "We'll be sure to tell you."

Maggie and Clarissa walked together to the small area set aside for the speaker. "Hi," the woman said, greeting the two girls. "Did you come to hear ghost stories?"

The girls nodded. "Are they scary?" Clarissa asked.

The woman shook her head. "Not too scary," she admitted, and then she lowered her voice. "I don't want to frighten too many people."

"My mom says you can't see ghosts," Maggie said. "That you tell other people's stories."

The woman leaned forward and lowered her voice. "Can I tell you a secret?" she asked.

The girls nodded again. "We love secrets."

"I've seen ghosts, but I really don't like to talk about it," she said. "It makes people uncomfortable, so I mostly tell stories about other people who can see ghosts."

"My mom is like that," Clarissa said. "I think you would like my mom. Her name is Mary O'Reilly."

Terri smiled and nodded. "I've heard of your mom," she said. "And I think I would like your mom, too."

"We're going to listen to your stories for little while, but then we have to go. Is that okay?" Maggie asked.

"That's perfectly okay," Terri replied. "Why don't you sit towards the back so you can slip out quietly when you need to."

"Okay, thanks," Clarissa said.

The girls listened to the storyteller for about ten minutes, sitting at the edge of their chairs as she told of local ghosts who haunted area venues. Then Maggie reached over and touched Clarissa's hand, almost causing her to jump out of her seat in fright. Maggie clapped a hand over her mouth to keep from laughing and then motioned with her head that they needed to go. They climbed out of their chairs and went in search of Kate, who was browsing through the music section.

"Mom," Clarissa whispered. "We're going to go out to the statue now."

Kate smiled down at them and nodded. "Okay, I'll be out there in about five minutes."

175

Letting themselves out of the door, the girls walked hand in hand around the front of the library to the small park area located just north of the building. A statue of two men on a raised platform stood in the middle of the park, and next to it, on a bench, their ghost friend from the library was waiting for them.

"There he is," Clarissa said, pointing with her other hand. "I can see him."

Maggie nodded. "He likes this place, too," she said. "Especially when it's crowded in the library."

"Good afternoon, ladies," the ghost friend said cordially. "It's a lovely day, isn't it?"

"It feels like Halloween outside," Clarissa said, and then she cocked her head in thought. "Do ghosts like Halloween?"

He smiled and nodded. "Yes, I believe we do," he said. "It gives us a chance to get out among the real people without being discovered."

"Do ghosts actually go out trick-or-treating?" Maggie asked.

"No, we don't need sweets," he said. "But I am sure that you would be surprised at how many of those you pass on the streets are not really who you suppose them to be."

Clarissa rubbed her arm. "That gave me goosebumps," she said.

He laughed. "Well, any good ghost story is supposed to give you goosebumps," he replied. "And will you be going trick-or-treating?"

"Yes," Maggie replied excitedly. "We're going to go together, and we're going to get enough candy to last until Christmas."

Clarissa nodded in agreement. "And we're not going to eat it all at the same time and get sick."

He chuckled, his deep laugh resonating in the space around them. "Well, that is an excellent plan," he said. "My favorite treat was candied apples. Do they still give those away?"

Maggie shook her head. "No, they can't," she said.

"They can't?" he asked. "Why not?"

"Because everything has to be wrapped up," Clarissa explained. "So bad guys can't make us sick."

He shook his head, and his face became somber. "There are those who would harm children with poisoned candy?" he asked.

"Yeah, but not lots of people," Maggie reassured him. "My dad says it's just a few asses that spoil it for everyone else."

Clarissa inhaled sharply. "Maggie, you're not supposed to say that word," she said.

The ghost chuckled again. "Clarissa is probably correct," he said. "But I must agree with your father's sentiment."

"Are you going to go trick-or-treating on Friday?" Clarissa asked him.

He smiled at her. "Yes, I might take these long legs of mine out for a walk," he said. "But if you see me, you mustn't make a fuss."

"Yeah, 'cause people get weird," Maggie agreed. "But we'll wave at you."

"And I will most assuredly wave back at you," he said.

Clarissa stared at him for a moment and then smiled. "I know who you are," she exclaimed, her eyes wide with excitement.

He smiled at her. "Well, I suppose now you know another secret about me."

"Um, would you like to go to a party?" Clarissa asked.

"I haven't been to a party in a number of years," he replied with a gentle smile.

"Well, we're having a party at our class at school," Maggie said. "And to make sure the party is educational, our teacher asked us to do reports on famous ghosts."

"And you're our famous ghost," Clarissa added. "But the other kids, they won't actually have a ghost there, just us. I mean, if you can come."

He looked from one hopeful face to the other. "Ladies, I will do my best," he said, and then he looked up. "And now it seems that your mother is coming for you. I bid you both a good afternoon."

"Bye," Clarissa said.

"See you on Friday," Maggie added.

"Girls, who were you talking to?" Kate asked.

"Just a nice ghost," Maggie said.

"Uh-huh," Clarissa agreed. "A really nice one."

"Well, of course you were," Kate said, shaking her head slightly. "Why do I even ask?"

Chapter Thirty-three

The small café in downtown Polo was nearly empty when Bradley and Mary entered it. Of course, it was well past the noon hour, and most people where back at work. "Hi, you want a menu?" the waitress asked them as they walked in.

Mary smiled and nodded. "That would be nice," she said. She'd finally gotten used to the familiar expression in small town restaurants where locals already knew what they wanted and didn't need a menu.

"Just take a seat anywhere," the woman replied. "My name's Viv, and I'll be back in a second to check on you."

Bradley led Mary to a booth that was wide enough for Mary's pregnant shape to slide into. "How are you doing?" he asked.

"I'm starving," she admitted. "I'm so glad you suggested we eat before we drive back to Freeport."

"You folks from Freeport?" Viv asked, setting two glasses of water down on the table.

"Yes," Bradley said. "We're just here for the day."

Viv pulled a notepad and pencil from the apron on her uniform, but then she paused, studying Mary. "You're Mary O'Reilly," she said. "The woman from the paper. The one who can see ghosts."

Mary nodded. "Yes, I am," she said.

"Did you hear that the police found Andrew Tyler's body in the basement of the old school?" she asked. "What a shame. He sure seemed like a nice fellow."

"Yes, he did," Mary replied, her private investigator instincts kicking in. "Did you know him?"

"Well, I'm a little bit older than he was," she said. "But I knew that teacher. The one he was investigating."

"Oh, you knew Kristen Banks," Mary said. "How did you know her?"

"We all went to high school together," she replied.

"That's what I love about small towns," Mary said. "You make friends in high school, and you stay friends even when you grow up." She paused for a moment and then pretended she had just thought of something. "Oh, we met someone else today. Um, Mitch. I think his name was Mitch…" she hedged, biting her lower lip for emphasis.

"Oh, Mitch Howse?" Viv asked.

"Yes, that's it," Mary said with a smile. "Mitch Howse. Did he go to school with you, too?"

Viv nodded. "Yeah, Mitch, my brother Vic, and Danny all served in Vietnam together."

"Serving together like that really creates strong bonds," Bradley said.

Viv nodded. "Yeah, it does," she agreed thoughtfully, and then she shook her head, as if to shake something off, and smiled down at them. "So, what can I get you?"

"A BLT sounds good to me," Mary said. "And I'd like fries and coleslaw."

"Got it," Viv said, scribbling it down. "How about you?"

"I'll have a cheeseburger and fries," he said.

"It comes with coleslaw," Viv reminded him. "And it's good coleslaw. I make it myself every morning."

"Oh, well then, I'll have some," he replied with a smile. "Thanks."

"Great," she said. "The food will be up soon. Can I get you anything to drink in the meantime?"

Mary shook her head. "No, water's fine for me," she said.

"Me, too," Bradley agreed.

They waited for her to walk back into the kitchen before they spoke again. "So, Mitch knew Kristen," Mary said. "That makes things a little more interesting."

Bradley nodded. "And he knew Danny, too," he added. "I wonder if he got home from his deployment before Danny."

"And I wonder if he was interested in Kristen," Mary added.

"Well, I can hunt down the military records for Mitch," Bradley offered.

"That would be great," Mary replied. "And then I can talk to Kristen and also go through her journal. It'll be very interesting to see if Mitch is part of her entries."

Bradley reached over and took Mary's hands in his. "The only thing I ask," he began, "is that you make sure you don't put yourself at risk. We know that whoever did this is not afraid to kill again to cover his tracks."

"Poor Andrew," Mary said. "All he wanted to do was solve an old mystery."

"That's the problem with mysteries in small towns," Bradley said.

"What?" Mary asked, leaning forward.

"Everyone knows what you're doing," he whispered. "And it's really hard to keep a secret."

Mary sat back when Viv came back into the room. She was carrying a cream pie in her hand. Placing it on the counter, she expertly sliced it up into eight perfect pieces. Lifting the cream-covered knife up, she turned to Mary. "Nothing like a sharp knife to get a job done," she said, carefully wiping it off on a red-checked dish cloth. "Can I save you a piece?"

"Is it banana cream?" Mary asked.

Viv nodded.

"No, don't save me a piece" Mary replied, and then she winked at Viv. "You should bring one over right now. I think today's one of those days when I definitely deserve dessert first."

"Two forks?" Viv asked, scooping a large piece out of the pan and placing it on a plate.

"Sure, I'll share," Mary replied. "As long as he takes the half with all the calories."

Chapter Thirty-four

Mary locked the door to her office and closed the blinds so she had a little privacy before she walked over to her desk and pulled out the journal and the stack of letters she'd found hidden away the night before. She sat down, sipping on a bottle of water, and then flipped through the journal to find the last page.

"Don't you think it's rude to go through someone else's journal?" Kristen asked, appearing next to her. "Without at least waiting for her to arrive."

"Not when I think it might help me discover who murdered her," Mary replied.

"Oh, good point," Kristen said. "So, what are you reading?"

Mary scanned the page. "A list of things for your wedding," she said, looking up. "You were really organized."

Shrugging, Kristen peered over Mary's shoulder. "Yeah, I was one of those people who always knew what she wanted and went for it," she said. "Who would have guessed I would end up on the wrong side of an iron banister?"

"I met someone today," Mary said as she continued to glance through the pages. "Actually two someones today. Mitch Howse and Viv... I don't think I got her last name."

"Viv Kutchens," Kristen said. "She and her twin brother were in my class."

"And Mitch?" Mary asked.

"Mitch. Mitch Howse," Kristen said with a smile. "He was always the nicest guy. For a while I actually considered dating him."

"Why didn't you?" Mary asked.

"Because he didn't fit the profile," she replied with a sigh.

"The profile?"

"Yeah, I was the head cheerleader, the prom queen, the homecoming queen," she said. "You know...the most popular girl in school. There were expectations about who I was supposed to marry."

"I take it Danny was the quarterback?" Mary guessed.

"Yeah. And the point guard for the basketball team, the shortstop for the baseball team and the lead in the school play," she listed off.

Mary looked up at her in surprise.

"It was a small school," Kristen explained.

"So, what was Mitch?" Mary asked.

"He was a linebacker in football, a forward for the basketball team and a catcher for the baseball team," she said. "And he built sets for the school play."

"Did you like him?" Mary asked.

"Yeah, but I liked a lot of boys," she admitted. "But Danny was the one I decided I was going to marry."

"So, Mitch and Danny both went to Vietnam?," Mary asked.

"Yeah, they were all the right age," she said, "so most of the boys from my class were drafted."

"Did Mitch get home before Danny?"

Kristen thought about the question for a moment. "Yes," she said slowly. "Yes, I remember that he got home a couple of weeks before I got the last letter from Danny."

"Which letter?" Mary asked.

"I tucked it into the journal on the night I died," she explained.

Mary flipped through the journal and found the slim airmail letter. "Is this it?" she asked, pulling it out and unfolding it on the table.

Kristen leaned forward and read the letter sitting on Mary's desk. Looking up, tears shining in her eyes, she nodded. "Yes," she whispered. "That was the last thing I read before I died."

She wiped her eyes, but the tears wouldn't stop. "I'm sorry, Mary," she whimpered. "I need to go. I'll come back, I promise."

Mary wiped the tears off her own cheeks as she watched Kristen fade away. "Don't worry about it," she whispered.

She picked up the journal, started reading it from the beginning, and gasped in shock. Then she began to laugh. She picked up her water bottle, took a sip and then propped her feet up on her desk. "Oh, Kristen, this is better than the movies," she said.

Chapter Thirty-five

"You want me to do what?" Bradley asked.

"It's not that hard," Kate said. "Just hang some sheets from this side of the wall and block off the kitchen and the dining room."

Rosie looked over her shoulder at the front door. "Are you sure Mary isn't going to walk in on us?" she asked. "I don't want her to be upset."

Bradley shook his head. "She promised she'd call before she left the office," he said. "So, we'll have at least ten minutes to get you out of here before she shows up. Now, back to me hanging my laundry across the house."

Kate laughed. "Come on, Bradley, it's not that hard," she said. "You just have to use thumb tacks and cordon off this area. Tell Mary you are planning a surprise for the family get-together, and she can't peek or it will be ruined."

He sighed and shook his head. "You know I'm not that guy," he said. "I'm the call-the-pizza-delivery-at-the-last-minute guy. She's going to get suspicious."

"Oh, I know," Rosie volunteered. "Tell her that Stanley said that he figured you would just call the pizza guy at the last minute, so you're doing this to show Stanley that he doesn't know what he's talking about."

"So this turns into it's about my honor, rather than I've suddenly started looking at that one website," he paused and thought for a moment. "Pin interest."

"Or something like that," Kate said. "But, yes, it's a challenge, and Stanley threw down the gauntlet."

"Yeah, I can go with that," he said. "So, what am I really doing?"

"You are really getting the sheets up by noon on Friday so Rosie and I can get in here and set things up," Kate replied.

"And, we are going to give you a list of things you have to buy and have in the refrigerator before we come," Rosie added.

"A list?" Bradley asked. "I don't know…"

"Oh, that's okay," Rosie said sweetly, waving the list in the air. "I told Stanley that if you couldn't do it, I'd give it to him…"

Bradley snatched the list out of her hand. "I'll take care of it," he said.

"You also have to remember to set all of the Halloween candy out in the front room so Mary doesn't have to go into the kitchen to replace it when it runs out," Kate reminded him.

"Why can't I put it all out in the bowl on the front porch?" he asked.

"Really?" Kate asked. "What would you do if you went trick-or-treating and someone put an entire cache of candy out, unguarded, on their front porch?"

"But I'm the chief of police," he argued.

"Then you should know better," Rosie said. "One bag of candy in the bowl, two shopping bags full of candy near the front closet ready for replenishment."

"And I still get to decorate the front porch, right?" he asked.

"Yes," Kate smiled. "Mary told us about the things you bought at the Halloween store. Clifford is jealous."

Bradley smiled. "Have him come over. He can help me set it up," he said. "I downloaded some special effects sounds, and I'm going to play them through Bluetooth speakers hidden under the coffins. I can't wait to scare people."

He paused and turned to Kate. "Um, when are your boys planning on stopping by?"

"Do you really want to start a war with the Brennan clan?" she asked. "They play for keeps."

191

"You're right," he agreed. "I want them on my side. Have them come over with Clifford, and they can help us set things up."

Rosie shook her head. "Just make sure you don't get all wrapped up in Halloween and forget what you're supposed to do for the shower," she cautioned.

"I promise, I won't," he said. "Besides, Mary is going to be so surprised. You two have outdone yourselves. She doesn't suspect a thing."

"That's the best part of a surprise shower," Rosie said. "The surprise."

"Now, the only thing that concerns me is this case she's working on," Kate said.

"Why does it concern you?" Bradley asked, suddenly tense.

"Well, I just want to be sure she's not going to be called away at the last minute and miss her own shower," Kate said.

"Oh, that," Bradley said, exhaling softly. "If she doesn't have it taken care of by the end of the week, I'll insist she take a break on Halloween night. Besides, with all of her family here, I'm sure that's what she's planning on doing anyway."

"Good," Rosie said with a satisfied sigh. "It all sounds like it's going to be perfect."

"Yes, it does," Kate said. "At this point, nothing could go wrong."

"Yeah, just remind me to knock on wood," Bradley said. "Just to be safe."

Chapter Thirty-six

Plywood scarecrows were propped up against streetlights and parking signs, signaling the celebration of fall in downtown Freeport. In the late evening hours, when the shops were closed and the traffic non-existent, the friendly figures transformed from harbingers of the harvest to dark specters lurking near shadowed signposts. But tonight, the wooden mannequins were actually treacherous because they hid within their number a true menace of the night seeking to silence a threat.

The soldier slipped from the alleyway and pressed a camouflaged jacket against the brick façade of the nearby building. The target was less than a click away, alone and unaware in her office. Shifting slightly, an object slipped from the sleeve of the jacket downwards. The cold steel of the knife felt familiar in the soldier's hand. It would only take a moment, and then the threat would be eliminated.

Taking a steadying breath, the shadowed figure turned and dashed up the side street, ducking for cover at the entrances of the closed downtown shops. A cursory glance down the street showed the only building with the glow of light from a street-level office was only half a block away. That had to be the target.

The soldier slipped to the next darkened entrance and waited. It wouldn't be long now. She would walk out of her office and turn to lock the door. That's when the attack would happen. It would be quick and professional. She would not suffer.

A car pulled down the street, and the soldier pushed back into the far corners of the entranceway, melting into the shadows. But instead of continuing down the block, the car pulled up in front of the target's office and beeped his horn.

"Hey, girlie," Stanley called, stepping out of his giant Buick. "Don't you know it's time for you to get yourself home?"

"Stanley, I was just leaving," Mary replied, walking out of her office and locking the door. "What are you doing out so late?"

"I just felt like I needed a ride in the night air," he replied.

Laughing, she walked over to his car. "Hmmmm, now why don't I believe that?" she asked.

He reached into his car and pulled out a container from the local ice cream shop. "Well, if you must know, I'm afraid I've developed a hankering for pumpkin pie shakes. But they had a two fer one deal, and you know how I can't pass up a deal," he confessed. "So iffen you want to stay on my good side, you'll take the one I bought for you and destroy the evidence."

"Pumpkin pie," she moaned. "Stanley, I ate banana cream pie at lunch."

"Well, it ain't lunch now," he said. "It's practically the next day, so it don't count."

She grinned at him and took the offered shake. "Well, who am I to argue with that kind of logic?" she asked, tasting the delicious treat. "Oh, Stanley, this is really good."

"Well, don't stand out on the street drinking it," he said, glancing down the street. "You never know when Rosie's going to drive by, and she'll chew my hide for eating sweets this late at night."

Mary opened her car door, put her purse and briefcase in the passenger's side and slipped behind the steering wheel. "Thank you, Stanley," she said. "I was actually getting hungry. You saved my life."

Stanley waved at her and slipped into his own car. "Anytime, girlie," he called. "You have a good night."

The soldier watched in irate silence as Mary drove away into the night. "Next time," the low voice throbbed with fury. "Next time you won't be so lucky."

Chapter Thirty-seven

Bradley stood on the front porch watching for Mary to drive up. He didn't want it to look like he was worried about her, but after the other night, he was. Looking up into the night sky he stared at the nearly full moon and the almost starless sky. Only the brightest stars could be seen when the moon was that bright.

"The other ones are there," Mike said, appearing next to him. "You just can't see them."

"So, you read minds now, too?" Bradley replied, still looking up to the sky and not giving Mike the satisfaction of knowing he'd startled him.

"Yeah, only simple ones," Mike teased. "They're easy."

Bradley chuckled. "So, what wise philosophical statement do you have for me tonight?" he asked, only half-joking. "That sometimes I don't see all the blessings I have because worry overshadows them? Or maybe I don't see the good in people because one bad trait blinds me to the others? Or perhaps I don't see all the tiny miracles that happen throughout my day because life overshadows them?"

Mike shrugged. "No, I was commenting on the stars," he said.

Bradley turned his head, looked at Mike and grinned. "You can be such an ass," he said.

"That's ass-angel to you," Mike countered, grinning back. "She's fine. Stanley stopped by with a pumpkin shake at just the right moment."

Bradley started to smile, then stopped and met Mike's eyes. "There was a potential wrong moment, then," he stated.

Mike nodded. "Yeah, there was."

"And did you have anything to do with Stanley's sudden urge for late night ice cream?" Bradley asked.

Once again, Mike shrugged. "Hey, I told you. I'm not supposed to interfere," he said. "But, you know, stuff happens."

"Thank you," Bradley said with sigh. "For not interfering in your own unique way."

"No problem," Mike replied. "But keep an eye on her. There's a troubled soul involved in this one."

"Who…" Bradley began, but before he could ask the question, Mike had already faded away. He sighed again. "Yeah, I know. You can't interfere."

Mary's car pulled up into the driveway, and Bradley jogged down the stairs towards the car. He was at her door before she was able to open it. "Hey," he said, opening the door for her and helping her out.

"Hey," she replied.

He covered her mouth with a kiss and held her in his arms, giving himself a moment to stop worrying about what Mike mentioned. Finally he released her. "Pumpkin?" he asked.

She grinned and reached back into the car for a half-filled container. "Stanley decided that neither of us could do without a pumpkin shake tonight," she explained. "But he bought a large. Who in the world can finish an entire large?"

"So what you're saying is that you're going to share?" Bradley asked hopefully.

She nodded and handed him the cup. "Yes, I am pumpkined-out."

He bent over to grab her purse and briefcase, handed them to her, then loosely placed his arm over her shoulders and walked her back to the house. "So, how was working late?" he asked, sipping on the shake.

"It was an interesting combination of paranormal and good, old-fashioned gossip," she said. "I started reading the journal and letters.

Kristen was there for a while, but the memories were too much for her."

"Find anything interesting?" he asked.

"Well, first, Polo is filled with interesting people according to Kristen, and she has definite views on just about everyone," Mary said with a soft laugh. "She's one of those people that you want to have as a friend, because as an enemy, she would be ferocious."

"Could that have gotten her killed?" he asked, opening the front door for her.

Mary shook her head as she placed her purse and briefcase down. "No, I think it was unrequited love," she said. "She has a number of love letters, even after she was engaged to Danny, trying to convince her that Danny wasn't the one for her."

They walked over to the couch and sat down. Mary propped her feet up on the ottoman and snuggled against Bradley. He put his arm around her shoulders and asked, "Was Mitch one of them?"

Mary nodded. "Yeah, Mitch and Victor," she said. "Kristen said Viv had a twin brother, so that must have been Vic."

"Viv, the waitress we had today?" he asked. "The one who said they all still hang around together."

200

"Yes," Mary said. "Kristen didn't say a great deal about her, but Kristen actually seemed like she would have been interested in Mitch if things had been different."

"I wonder if he felt that way, too, and decided to force the issue," Bradley mused, sucking the last drops from the bottom of the cup and making a terrible noise.

Mary grinned up at him. "Are you done?" she asked.

He smiled at her. "I suppose it would be fairly gauche if I took the top off and licked the rest off the sides?" he asked.

She nodded. "Yes. Yes, it would," she said and chuckled softly. "So, how was Clarissa tonight?"

"She was great," he said, leaning into her contentedly. "She was working on her school project."

"Oh, what's it on?" Mary asked.

He shook his head. "Nope, it's top secret," he said. "She wants to surprise you when you come to her class on Friday."

"Well, I can't wait to be surprised," Mary said, and then she yawned widely.

Leaning over, Bradley placed a kiss on her forehead. "Well, first sleep and then surprise, okay?" he said, standing up and offering her his hands.

She let him pull her out of the couch and then wrapped her arms around his waist, laying her head on his chest. "Thanks for being my partner today," she murmured.

He hugged her and placed his head on hers. "Cutest partner I ever had," he said. "I think we make a good team."

She smiled up at him. "I totally agree."

Chapter Thirty-eight

Mary hung up the phone and smiled as Bradley walked into her office the next morning. "Good morning," she said. "Perfect timing."

"Good, I have news for you," he said, sliding into the chair across from her desk. "I was able to get hold of the military discharge reports for Mitch Howse."

"And?" Mary asked.

"He got home about two weeks before Kristen's death," he replied. "It sounds like he might have been injured, but nothing that would have prevented him from attacking Kristen."

"Well, I just got off the phone with Daniel Toba, Kristen's old fiancé," she explained. "He's willing to meet with me…"

Bradley frowned at her. "Mary…"

"Here in Freeport, in my office, in the middle of the day," she finished quickly. "Okay?"

The frown turned into a slightly abashed smile. "Yeah, okay," he said. "That was nice of him."

"Well, when I explained what happened to Andrew, he decided he wanted to cooperate in every way possible," she said.

"Great," Bradley said. "If you need me to come over and sit in, just call."

"I will," she said, leaning back in her chair and tucking her hands behind her head. "And now we have to discuss something really serious."

"Yes?" he asked.

"Your Halloween costume," she said. "What are you going to wear?"

"Costume?" he asked. "Mary, I'm not going anywhere. Your family is coming over to tell stories. I'll be answering the door and giving children candy. I think a t-shirt and jeans are a perfect costume."

"Bradley, it's only once a year," she said. "How often do you get to wear a costume?"

"I wear a costume every day," he replied.

She shook her head. "No, that's a uniform, not a costume," she said. "You need a costume."

"How about one of those t-shirts that say, "This is my…""

"A costume," she interrupted her tone brooking no argument.

"What are you going to be wearing?" Bradley demanded.

"Rosie is getting a costume for me," she replied. "I'm going to be a gypsy."

He paused and a smile grew on his face. "With one of those elasticy kind of necklines that slip down over your shoulders?"

"Could be," she said with a returning smile.

He sighed. "Okay, Rosie did mention something about a matching costume for me," he admitted. "But it was a little silly – calf-high pants and a vest. That was it, not even a shirt."

"You as a gypsy," Mary said, picturing the outfit he described on her hunky husband. "Yeah, that could be nice."

"Okay, I'll wear the vest as long as you wear the nibble and nudge blouse," he said.

"Nibble and nudge?" she asked, raising her eyebrows.

He actually blushed and shrugged awkwardly. "Yeah, you know, you nibble on the exposed skin and then you kind of, um, nudge the material down."

She laughed out loud. "Bradley Alden!" she said in mock censure.

"Yes, Mary Alden?" he asked, smiling at her.

She sighed. "I can't wait until Halloween."

He nodded. "Yeah, my feelings about Halloween just went up a couple of notches."

Chapter Thirty-nine

Danny looks just like his photos on his social media page, Mary thought as he entered her office later that morning.

"Hi, I'm Daniel," he said, looking a little confused. "Are you Mary O'Reilly?"

Mary walked over and shook his hand. "Yes, I am," she said. "Why?"

He shrugged. "I don't know," he said. "I guess I didn't expect a private investigator to be, you know, pregnant."

"Oh," she replied, looking down at her stomach. "Well, I guess it happens to the best of us." She looked up with a smile and met his eyes. "But don't worry, I can still think rationally. At least for a couple more weeks."

Looking more than a little confused, he shook his head. "So, you do want to interview me, right?" he asked.

"Okay, so he was never the sharpest knife in the drawer," Kristen said, appearing next to him. "But he looked really good in a uniform."

"I do want to interview you," she paused. "Daniel?"

"Danny, please, everyone calls me Danny."

"Okay, Danny, have a seat," Mary said, motioning to a chair on the other side of her desk. "Would you like something to drink? Water? A soda?"

"No, I'm good," he replied, slipping into the chair. "I just want to know what's going on. I mean Kristy died a long time ago."

"Kristen," Kristen corrected. "I hated Kristy."

"I know it was a long time ago," Mary said. "But new information has come to light that makes it seem like it might not have been the accident everyone assumed it was."

He leaned forward. "Are you saying she was murdered?" he asked.

"Would it have mattered?' Kristen asked. "Would you have maybe put your marriage to Janice off another month or so?"

Mary took a deep breath and smiled at Danny. "Well, we don't know exactly what happened," Mary said. "But we know that she wasn't alone when she died."

"Oh, that's good," he said, nodding his head. "I mean, I've heard that people don't like to be alone when they die."

"No," Mary said, shaking her head. "I mean someone might have pushed her down the stairs."

"Oh, well, that's not good," he said.

"Okay, he wasn't even close to being a sharp knife," Kristen said with an exaggerated sigh. "He was more like a spoon."

"So, what we're trying to do is piece together what happened around the time of her death," Mary said.

"Well, I was still in Nam when she died," he replied, starting to stand up. "So, I don't know how much help I can be."

"And we're done," Kristen added.

Mary reached over and placed her hand on his arm. "Well, actually I think you could have more information than you realize."

"Oh, yeah? How?" he asked, sitting back down.

"When you finally arrived home, did you notice anyone acting differently towards you?" Mary asked.

"Different?"

"Sometimes guilt can be manifested in a variety of ways. For example, someone who might have once been a mutual friend could avoid you if they felt guilty. And, on the other hand, someone you barely knew could suddenly try and act like your best friend. Any of those changes in personality could be a clue."

Danny nodded. "Oh, hey, yeah, that's pretty cool. Like one of those psychologist things on television," he said. "Let me think."

He paused for a few moments, looking down at his hands while he concentrated. "I thought about it," he said, raising his head and meeting Mary's eyes. "And you know, Mitch, Mitch Howse, he was never the same after I came home. I don't know. I tried to get together with him and Viv, but they wouldn't have anything to do with me."

"Is there any other reason they wouldn't get together with you?" Mary asked.

"Well, you know, Mitch almost died over there," he said. "And I came home pretty much blemish free. I always thought he was just jealous of me. But, you know, it could have been that."

"Well, really, facing death could change someone," Mary suggested.

"Yeah, but I could never figure out why Viv was his friend but she wasn't friends with me," Danny said.

"Why wouldn't Viv be his friend?" Mary asked.

"Because Viv's twin brother died saving Mitch's life," Danny said.

"What?" Mary asked.

"Yeah, they were under fire, and Mitch got pinned down in the jungle," Danny explained. "Their captain ordered the rest of them to retreat, said it was too late for the ones in the swamp. But Vic didn't want to leave Mitch, so he disobeyed orders and ran back into the jungle, his machine gun blazing. They said he took out a couple dozen Vietcong before they got him. After all the smoke died down, the rest of the platoon was able to go in and rescue the guys, including Mitch, but it was too late for Vic."

"Oh, that's awful," Mary said. "I'm sure that it was devastating for Vic's whole family."

Danny shrugged. "Well, it was just Vic and Viv," he said. "Their dad left when they were born. Their mom told them he couldn't handle two babies at the same time. Then their Mom died when they were in high school."

"Best thing that could have happened to them," Kristen muttered. "That woman was a crazy bitch. Blamed them both for the hardships in her life."

"So, Viv got a little money from the government because of Vic's death, and she bought the café," he said. "Some people might have thought

211

it was blood money, and some people might have said that. But what choice did she have?'

"People actually said that?" Mary asked, incredulous.

"And you thought I was bad," Kristen said. "At least I had the decency to only write my thoughts down and not say them out loud."

"Yeah, they said it," he said with a shrug. "But Viv's always been strong. She can take it."

Chapter Forty

"Viv, I really need you to be strong," Mitch said as they sat alone in the café. The sign had been turned to "CLOSED," and the shades had been pulled down to block the midday sun. Mitch pushed the plate with a half-eaten piece of pie away from him. "We need to talk about this."

"Mitch, I don't understand," she said. "Kristen's death was a long time ago. Why bring it up now?"

"Because Andrew Tyler was also killed," Mitch said.

Viv nodded. "I heard," she said, purposely keeping herself busy behind the counter. "They found his body in the school. And that's a shame. He seemed like such a nice young man."

"But Viv, you need to listen to me," Mitch insisted. "He was murdered."

"It's not like I'm unsympathetic," Viv said, looking up from shelving some coffee cups. "But what does that have to do with us? We don't know what kind of stuff he was involved with in Chicago. I figured his life just caught up with him."

Mitch stood up and paced to the door of the café and back. "Don't you get it?" he said, trying to keep his frustration in check. "It didn't have anything to do with Chicago. I *know* it didn't. Do you understand?"

Staring at him, she came around the counter and walked to him, placing her hands on his arms. "Mitch, are you saying you know who killed Andrew?" she asked, meeting his eyes.

He stared at her for a moment and then dropped his head. "Yes. Yes, I know who killed Andrew," he replied, his voice filled with incredible sorrow.

"Oh, Mitch," Viv said, sliding her hands up his arms and embracing him. "I won't tell. I promise. It will be just our secret."

Placing his hands on her shoulders, he gently pushed her back. "But that wouldn't be right, would it?" he asked. "It wouldn't be right to lie about what happened, would it?"

She sighed and tears glistened in her eyes. "I know that things changed after you came back from Nam," she said. "And I know that all of us were changed when Vic died. And back then, they didn't understand things like post-traumatic stress disorder, so we all just stumbled through life."

"But that doesn't give us the right to kill someone," he said. "Even if we feel our secrets are going to be revealed, it still doesn't give us that right."

She shook her head, stepped away from him and walked back to the counter. "Kristen's death was an accident," she said. "I know it was an accident."

She felt his hands on her shoulders once again. "But this time," he whispered, "this time it wasn't."

"No, you're right," she agreed. "This time it was deliberate, to cover up the secret from so long ago."

He exhaled harshly. "And how many have to die to cover up the past?" he asked. "I thought it was only a one time occurrence. I thought I had it all handled..."

A tear slipped down her cheek. "Are you..." she faltered. "What are you going to do?"

He turned her and pulled her into his arms for a comforting embrace. "I'm going to go down to the police department and confess," he said. "And I have to do it before that woman Mary O'Reilly gets any more information on the case. If Mary testifies, it will cause more trouble than we can imagine. Besides, I know Vic would want me to do it."

She shook her head and looked at him. "Vic would want you to be happy," she said. "That's the most important thing. You don't have to do this. You don't have to worry about Mary O'Reilly."

He placed a chaste kiss on her forehead. "Yes, I do," he said. "Goodbye, Viv. Take care of yourself."

Chapter Forty-one

"So, then there's this knock on the door," Stanley said, sitting at his kitchen table watching Kate and Rosie create cheesecakes. "But, I can see straight out the window, and there ain't no one on the door stoop doing the knocking."

Kate paused from pressing chocolate cookie crumbs into the bottom of a spring-form pan and turned to Stanley. "Are you kidding me?" she asked.

"Scout's honor," Stanley said, raising his hand to form the familiar sign. "'Tweren't hide nor hair of anyone even close to that door."

"So, what did you do?" Kate asked, returning to her task.

"I called my older sister's name and told her someone was waiting at the door fer her," he chuckled. "I figured if anyone could scare away a ghostie, it would have been Lenora."

"Stanley," Rosie scolded. "As I recall, Lenora was a lovely woman."

"Well, yeah, she mellowed in her old age," he replied. "But as a youngster, she pinched my ear so many times my left ear was a full inch longer than my right one."

Kate chuckled and then wiped her hands off on a dish towel. "Okay, Rosie, here's step one," she said. "How does it look?"

Coming up next to her, Rosie critically eyed the baking pan filled with the chocolate crust. "It looks perfect," Rosie said. "And delicious. Now put it in the oven for about five minutes, to set it. And while it's baking, you can melt the chocolate over the double-boiler."

"Okay," Kate replied. "I am so grateful that you are helping me with this."

"Oh, it's my pleasure," Rosie said. "It's nice to have company while I'm baking."

"I'm always here when you're baking," Stanley interjected. "What am I, chopped liver?"

Rosie shook her head. "No, you're a nuisance," she replied. "A sweet nuisance."

He stood up, walked over to where Rosie was creating her cheesecake and stuck his finger in the batter bowl. He popped the batter in his mouth and nodded happily. "It's good," he said. "What is it? Something with cinnamon?"

Rolling her eyes, Rosie shooed him away from the mixer. "Stanley Wagner, you step away from my work area," she said. "It's pumpkin cheesecake, if you must know, and it's for tomorrow night."

Grumbling, Stanley moved away from the mixer. "A man could starve in his own house," he muttered, moving back towards the table.

Kate sent Rosie a quick grin, and Rosie shook her head. "There are some fresh oatmeal raisin cookies in the cookie jar," she said. "I made them this morning because I knew you'd be prowling around the kitchen getting in my way."

He hurried over to the counter, pulled the lid off the cookie jar and inhaled deeply. "Rosie, my love, you are amazing," he said, lifting out four cookies.

"Two," she said. "After that shake last night, you don't need four cookies."

Stanley glanced over at her, dropped one cookie back in the jar and slid the extra one into his pocket. "I'm just gonna take a little drive downtown," he said.

"That's a wonderful idea," Rosie agreed. "And while you're out, would you mind dropping that box off at Mary's office? It's her costume for tomorrow."

"Well, then I probably need a couple more cookies for Mary," he said, lifting the lid off the jar once again. "You know she's eating for two."

"I'm going to call Mary and make sure she got those cookies," Rosie warned Stanley.

He grabbed a handful of cookies and turned to Rosie with a smile. "She'll get them all right," he said, and then added with a grin. "Leastways she'll tell you she got them."

Rosie shook her head once he was gone. "That man," she said with a huff.

"You totally adore him," Kate said.

Rosie smiled. "Yes, I really do," she said. And then she stopped and clapped her hand over her mouth. "You don't think he'll mention to Mary that we were baking together?"

Kate slipped the double-boiler from the heated element to the middle of the stove. "Oh, call him, quickly," she said.

They both hurried over to the counter, and Rosie picked up her cell phone. As soon as she dialed, they both heard a phone ringing in the living room. With a sigh, Rosie shook his head. "He forgot his phone," she said. "Again."

"Well, there's nothing we can do about it now," Kate said, going back to her melted chocolate. "I will sure be glad when this shower is over. I never realized how hard it would be to keep this whole thing a secret."

"Well, perhaps he won't tell her," Rosie said. "You know, he did some top secret work when he was in the military. He does know how to keep a secret."

Kate turned, met her eyes and raised one eyebrow.

"You're right," Rosie said. "He's going to spill the beans as soon as he walks through the door."

Kate nodded. "We could always call Bradley and have him cut Stanley off at the pass," she suggested.

"Oh, that's a wonderful idea," Rosie said, picking up her phone again. "And Bradley will be happy to shut Stanley up."

Chapter Forty-two

Stanley pulled his car into a parking spot about a half-block away from Mary's office. Grabbing the box and the cookies, he stepped out of his car and started toward the sidewalk.

"Stanley!"

He turned to see Bradley hurrying down the street to meet him. "Dagnabbit, did that woman call the police because of a couple of oatmeal cookies?" he grumbled.

Laughing, Bradley shook his head. "No, she called me because you forgot your phone at the house, and she needed to remind you not to mention to Mary that she and Kate were together," he said.

"I don't need reminding," Stanley growled. "I got a mind like a steel trap." He pointed a finger to his head. "Ain't nothing gonna slip past this mind."

"Well good," Bradley said. "Then we don't have to worry."

They walked together down the street to Mary's office.

"Well, to what do I owe the honor of having two such handsome men come into my office?" Mary asked.

"I got shooed out of my house," Stanley said. "So I'm delivering cookies and a costume."

He walked over to her desk, put the box on a clear corner and handed her the bag of cookies.

"Well, I'm sorry you got shooed out," she said, opening the plastic bag. "But I'm excited about the delivery. Thank you, Stanley."

"Well, iffen you think that's too many cookies," he said, "I would be happy to help you eat them."

She grinned and held out the bag for him and Bradley. "But let's keep this our little secret," Mary said. "I wouldn't want Rosie to think that I didn't appreciate her baking."

"Oh, well, she's in baking heaven right now," Stanley said as he happily munched on the cookie. "She's getting to play mother hen, teaching Kate Brennan how to bake..."

He froze, half a cookie hanging from his mouth, and swallowed loudly.

"Steel trap, eh?" Bradley whispered to him.

"Kate's over at Rosie's?" Mary asked. "And they're baking together?"

Suddenly, Bradley's phone rang. *Saved by the bell*, he thought. He pulled it out and looked at the

223

caller ID. "It's the Polo Police Department," he said as he clicked on the phone to answer it.

"Alden," he said into the receiver. He remained silent, although his eyebrows rose in surprise. "You don't say."

"What?" Mary whispered. "What don't you say?"

He covered the mouthpiece with his hand. "Mitch just turned himself in."

Mary sat back in her chair, and her jaw dropped. "He confessed?" she said. "Well, I would have never in a million years…"

"Yes, thank you," Bradley said. "I really appreciate the call."

Disconnecting the phone, he shook his head. "Why does this bother me so much?" he asked.

"Because we didn't get to solve the crime," Mary said with a shrug. "It's a bit of a letdown."

Nodding slowly, Bradley thought about that for a minute. "Well, he was my favorite suspect," he said.

"Mine, too," Mary agreed. "He had opportunity and motive. And Danny told me that Mitch had stopped hanging around with him once he got back from Vietnam."

"Why are you two fussing?" Stanley asked, grateful the focus had shifted from his gaffe. "You got the crime solved, and now you can enjoy Halloween without worrying."

Mary nodded. "Well, that's true," she said. "There's just something…"

"Yeah," Bradley said with a shrug. "Something. But, maybe it's just that Mitch snatched the victory lap away from us."

"Okay, I can admit that I love the victory lap," Mary said with a smile. "So, no mystery, and we can enjoy Halloween. I like that!"

Mary turned to Stanley and held open the bag of cookies. "Well, let's celebrate," she said. "Cookies all around."

"Actually, girlie," Stanley said, backing away from her desk. "I'd best be on my way. Rosie's probably looking fer me. Can't keep her waiting."

"Are you sure?" Mary asked.

Stanley nodded. "Sure as sure can be," he said with a quick nod as he let himself out the door.

"A rat abandoning the ship," Bradley muttered, turning and watching through the window as Stanley made his way down the street.

"What did you say?" Mary asked.

Bradley turned back to Mary and smiled. "Oh, nothing important," he replied, and then he picked up the box. "So, let's take a look at this costume."

"Don't change the subject," she said sadly.

"What subject?" Bradley asked, inwardly praying that it was not the subject he thought it was going to be.

"Rosie and Kate are baking together," she said softly.

Damn, it was that subject.

"Yes, they are," he replied, taking another bite of cookie. "And it sounds like Rosie was giving Kate tips, just like Rosie used to do for you before we were married."

Mary looked up at him, surprised. "But, they didn't…" she began.

Bradley leaned over and placed his hands on the edge of her desk. "Mary, I really don't want to upset you," he said. "But when are you going to stop thinking the worst of your friends and start trusting them again."

She sat back quickly as if she'd been slapped. "I don't think the worst…" she started.

His raised eyebrow silenced her. She was quiet for a long moment, and finally she sighed. "I haven't given them the benefit of the doubt, have I?" she asked quietly.

He shook his head.

"I've been a bit of a brat, haven't I?"

He leaned over farther and kissed her lips lightly. "No, you have been on a roller coaster of emotions," he said. "And we all know it. And we all love you."

"What should I do?" she asked.

"Worry less and have more fun," he replied.

She laughed softly. "That's what Mike told me to do," she said.

"Mike's a genius," Bradley replied with a smile.

Pushing back her chair, she stood up and walked around her desk. "I have no more work for the day," she said with a teasing smile. Then she picked up the box and held it to her chest. "Want to come home and help me try on my costume?"

He leaned over the box and kissed her again. "And you're a genius, too."

Chapter Forty-three

"I can't believe it's Halloween!" Clarissa shouted as she ran down the stairs the next morning. "This is going to be the greatest day ever!"

Mary smiled at Bradley. "And she hasn't even had sugar yet," she whispered.

"Can we have waffles for breakfast this morning?" Clarissa asked.

"No," Mary said, grabbing her excited daughter and pulling her close for a hug. "You are going to have a day filled with sugar. So, breakfast is bacon and eggs."

"Bacon and eggs sound good, too," Clarissa agreed with a smile.

"Or we could have hotdogs," Mike said as he appeared in the kitchen. "But we would have to have holes cut through them."

"Why?" Clarissa asked.

"Because then they would be hollow-weenies," he joked.

"Oh, that was really bad," Mary chuckled, rolling her eyes.

"That joke was so bad that it almost made my stomach hurt," Clarissa added.

"Of course, we all know what you're having for lunch," Bradley said, getting into the spirit of the game.

"What?" Mary asked, more than a little worried about his answer.

"Boo-logna sandwiches," he said. Mike floated over and high-fived him.

"With ice scream for dessert," Mike said to Bradley.

Bradley laughed and nodded. "Or frankenfurters with ketchup," Bradley said.

"Or, if you want Mexican, you could always have a boo-rito," Mike said, laughing with Bradley.

Mary and Clarissa looked at each other and shook their heads. "They're scarier than Halloween," Clarissa whispered.

"I agree," Mary said. "Perhaps if we just ignore them."

"Bradley," Mike said, "where do mummies go for a swim?"

"The dead sea," Bradley replied. "Mike, where does a vampire keep his money?"

"A blood bank," Mike answered in his best Dracula imitation. "What do birds sing on Halloween?"

Bradley paused. "I don't know? What?"

"Twick or tweets."

Clarissa looked from Bradley and Mike to Mary. "Are these supposed to be funny jokes?" she asked.

"Ouch," Bradley said. "You just thrust a sword of scorn right through my heart."

"Or a sword of good taste," Mary said, sending an apologetic smile in the direction of her husband. "Just saying."

"Wow. Et tu, Mary?" Bradley asked.

Laughing, she shook her head. "While I would *love* to hear more Halloween puns, we've got to get moving. After breakfast, Clarissa has to get into her costume and makeup before the bus comes."

"Okay," Mike replied with a sigh. "But we were just getting good."

Mary looked at him and shook her head. "Oh, no, you were both a long way from good."

Bradley chuckled and shook his head at Mike. "Tough audience," he said, picking up a plate, filling

230

it for Clarissa and placing it on the table before her. "Happy Halloween, sweetheart."

"Thanks, Dad," she said. Picking up a piece of bacon, she took a bite out of it and then pointed it in Mary's direction. "When are you coming to the school?"

"I'm supposed to be there by 10:30," Mary replied. "And then I get to listen to the special reports you did. And after that, we have a party."

"This is the most exciting day ever," Clarissa said. "I can't wait 'til you see my report. I worked really, really hard."

"I'm sure you did," Mary said. "And I know I'm going to be impressed."

Clarissa giggled. "Yes, you are going to be more impressed than anyone else in the classroom," she said.

"What do you mean by that?" Mary asked.

"You'll see," Clarissa said.

Mary turned to Bradley. "Are you sure you can't come?" she asked.

He shook his head regretfully, thinking about all of the things he had to get ready for the party while Mary was at the school. "I'm really sorry. I've got meetings all day."

"Well, we'll miss you," she replied. "And somehow you got away with not wearing a costume all day."

Bradley grinned. "Well, imagine that."

Chapter Forty-four

"Okay, I feel a little ridiculous," Mary said, standing in front of the mirror in her bedroom and looking at her reflection. The wide gypsy skirt and lace shawl camouflaged her growing baby bump, and the white peasant blouse set off what little tan she had left from the summer.

"I think you look sexy," Bradley said, coming up behind her and wrapping his arms around her waist before pressing a kiss to her neck.

"I'm going to be a room mother for a fourth grade Halloween party," she said. "I'm not supposed to be sexy."

"Says who?" Bradley asked. "I speak for fourth grade boys everywhere when I say that sexy moms are the best ones to have for room mothers."

She rolled her eyes. "Bradley, you're not helping," she said. "This is my first big event for Clarissa, and I don't want to embarrass her."

"First, you won't embarrass her. She is thrilled beyond belief that you are coming," he said. "Second, you look like a gypsy princess, not like a tramp. Your skirt is nearly to your ankles, and your blouse and shawl pretty much cover up everything else. Your costume is very appropriate. It's the woman inside the costume that's so sexy." He kissed her neck again. "Besides, I know what lurks beneath this demure outfit."

She smiled at him through the mirror. "Are you sure?" she asked.

"Positive," he said.

"Okay," she said, taking a deep breath. "Well then, wish me luck. I've never dealt with an entire classroom of over-sugared fourth graders."

"Just think of it like riot duty," he said. "And you'll be fine."

Chuckling, she turned and kissed him. "Thank you," she replied. "Excellent advice."

The classroom was already buzzing with excitement when Mary entered the room, her arms filled with shopping bags full of treats.

"Oh, good, Mrs. Alden, you're here," Mrs. Spangler said. "Perfect timing. We are just about to start our reports. Why don't you join Mrs. Brennan in the back of the room."

"Thank you," Mary said.

She hurried to the back of the room where Kate sat at the wooden table. She was dressed as a witch, and Mary felt a twinge of guilt. "Hi," Kate whispered, standing up and giving Mary a hug. "You look amazing."

"Thanks," Mary whispered. "Rosie picked it out for me."

"She's amazing," Kate said softly.

"I want to thank you for bringing the girls to the library so they could work on their project," Mary said in a hushed tone as they sat down next to each other.

"My pleasure," Kate replied. "I can't wait to see what they came up with."

"Now students," Mrs. Spangler began. "And moms," she added, acknowledging Mary and Kate with a nod of her head. "I am very excited to hear your reports. I know that you've been working so hard on them. So, first we'll let you introduce the main character of your report, tell a little bit about him or her, and then we'll let the class ask you questions."

She looked down at her clipboard. "Rusty, you're first."

"Isn't he the boy who throws up?" Mary asked.

Kate nodded. "But this isn't math, so we should be safe."

A tall, young boy with brown, curly hair and a shy smile stepped forward. "My report is on Resurrection Mary, a famous ghost in Chicago."

Mary and Kate listened with fascination as Rusty explained the legend and then read some eye-witness accounts of people who had actually picked up the hitchhiking ghost on Archer Avenue. After a few questions from his classmates, encouraged by the teacher, he sat down.

"Now, it's time for Maggie and Clarissa to give us their report," Mrs. Spangler said.

Maggie and Clarissa carried two poster boards to the front of the room and placed them in the easels Mrs. Spangler had provided. Then they moved into the center of the room, in front of the teacher's desk, and held hands.

"Oh, isn't that adorable?" Kate whispered to Mary. "They are holding hands."

Mary was about to answer when she noticed a movement in the doorway of the classroom. A tall, familiar-looking, well-dressed ghost in a black stovepipe hat walked through door and stood next to Maggie and Clarissa. Clarissa looked up at him and then looked directly at Mary with a wide smile on her face.

"Our report," Maggie began, and then Clarissa joined her, "is about President Abraham Lincoln."

Chapter Forty-five

"Mr. Lincoln," Mary said softly, keeping her voice low so others couldn't hear her. "It's an honor to meet you, sir."

She was in the corner of the room with her back facing the class as she prepared treat bags for the children. It was the perfect opportunity to speak with the president without having anyone think she was talking to herself.

He smiled at her. "It is my honor, my lady," he replied. "I assume that you are Miss Clarissa's mother. The one who can see ghosts, too?"

She smiled and nodded. "Yes, I am," she said.

"You must be very proud of these enterprising young ladies," he said, looking over to where the girls were mingling with their friends.

"Yes, I am," she said. "But I'm afraid I'm slightly confused. I had heard your spirit was often seen at the White House, but I'm surprised to see you in Freeport."

"Ah, well, Freeport holds an important place in my heart," he replied. "When I was a young captain in the Illinois militia, one of my first duties was to come here to the Freeport area during the Blackhawk Wars. I never engaged in battle, but I was a part of the militia that buried the soldiers that had fought. I was only twenty-three years old, but the memory of those who died stays with me even to this day."

"I had no idea," Mary said.

"Well, that is not my only connection to Freeport," he said. "In Freeport, I debated Stephen A. Douglas for the office of senator. As a matter of fact, the debate site is adjacent to the very library where I have engaged in delightful conversation with Miss Maggie and Miss Clarissa."

"And how did you do in the debate?" Mary asked.

A smile slowly grew on his face. "Let me just say that it was an election which I most assuredly lost."

Mary chuckled. "Well, it doesn't seem that Freeport holds very good memories," she said.

"Ah, but you don't know the rest of the story," he said, his eyes twinkling with enjoyment.

"And what would that be?" she asked.

"During the debate, I asked Douglas about his stance on slavery, whether territories had the right to determine if they were going to be free or slave states, or if, as according to a majority decision of the United States Supreme Court, the territories could not

238

legally exclude slavery." He chuckled. "That put the "little giant" in quite a quandary. He greatly respected the Supreme Court, but their decision was contrary to his political aspirations. He answered that despite what the court said, slavery could be prevented from any territory by the refusal of the people living in that territory to pass laws favorable to slavery. So, although he won the Senate contest, the Freeport Doctrine, as it was called, did not endear him to the people in the southern states. And that, I believe, was his downfall during the presidential election of 1860. The election that I won."

"You and Douglas must not have been on very good speaking terms after that," Mary suggested.

His smiled turned sober, and he slowly shook his head. "No, as a matter of fact, Stephen was a good man and a great supporter of my presidency, and he was one of the fiercest advocates of maintaining the Union." Meeting Mary's eyes, he smiled sadly. "He was my friend."

Mary was about to ask him another question when she heard her name called from the other side of the room. "Mrs. Alden," Mrs. Spangler called. "Would you like to join us in the parade around the school?"

Mary turned and smiled. "Of course, I would be delighted," she said, and when she turned back, President Lincoln was gone.

239

"He does that," Maggie said, both girls coming up alongside Mary. "But he always comes back."

Mary smiled down at them. "Well, that's good to know," she said.

"Were you surprised?" Clarissa asked. "Were you so surprised?"

"I was incredibly surprised," she said, bending over and giving Clarissa a hug and then turning and giving Maggie one, too. "I couldn't believe it when I saw him walking through the door."

"And I saw him," Clarissa said. "I actually saw a ghost."

Mary smiled at her, her heart melting at the joy in her daughter's face. "Yes you did," she said. "And I can tell that both of you made quite an impression on him."

"Clarissa, Maggie, take your place in line," Mrs. Spangler said.

"Oh, we have to go," Clarissa said, but then she gave Mary one more hug. "Thanks for coming to the party."

"I wouldn't have missed it for the world," she said.

With Kate in the lead, the classroom marched out into the hallway towards the doors to the playground. Mary waited as they left the room, taking up the back.

"Mrs. Alden," Mrs. Spangler said once the children had left the room. "I've been meaning to speak with you about Clarissa, and I put it off because I knew you would be here today."

"Oh?" Mary said, a pit growing in her stomach. "Is something wrong?"

"Well, I'm not sure," the teacher said, motioning to Mary to walk with her as they followed the children at a safe enough distance that they could see them but not be overheard. "It seems that Clarissa has had a strong interest in death lately."

"Death?" Mary asked.

The teacher nodded. "Yes, she asked me several times this week if anyone either died in this classroom, or in the gym, or in the lunchroom," she sighed. "Basically any place in the school we've gone."

The pit in Mary's stomach dissolved, and she smiled at the teacher. "Did you happen to catch the article in the paper about my work a couple of weeks ago?" Mary asked.

Mrs. Spangler shook her head. "No, I live in Rockford, so I don't subscribe to the local paper. Is it relevant to our discussion?"

"Actually, not really," Mary said, "but it might have shed a little more light on our families predilection to death or, more specifically, ghosts."

"I'm sorry?" Mrs. Spangler asked.

"It would seem that Clarissa has been more occupied with ghosts than death," Mary explained. "Other than her school project, my family has a tradition of telling ghost stories on Halloween night. Usually…" she paused to find the right word, "unique stories. So I'm sure that Clarissa was just trying to see if she could find a *real* ghost story."

Mrs. Spangler chuckled. "Children have the most outrageous imaginations, don't they? Real ghosts. How absurd."

Mary looked up ahead at the children, saw the tall, gangly former president walking in the midst of them, and shook her head. "How absurd indeed."

Chapter Forty-six

"Dammit," Bradley growled as he hit his thumb with the hammer for the third time. "This is not working."

"Not much to hanging a sheet up against a wall," Stanley muttered. "Most intelligent people could handle it."

Bradley turned slowly from his position on the top rung of the step ladder and glowered at Stanley. "Well then, why don't you try it?" he asked.

"Don't mind if I do," Stanley said, reaching up for the hammer and then stepping out of the way so Bradley could get down.

With a shrug, Bradley climbed down and stepped to the side while Stanley climbed up the ladder, smiling with a cocky certainty that he was going to show Bradley a thing or two. He placed the white sheet against the plaster wall, reached over and pulled a small, gold finishing nail from the container and set its point against the sheet. Applying pressure with his forearm to hold the sheet in place and gripping the nail between his thumb and forefinger, he brought the hammer down with exacting precision. The hammer hit the nailhead, and the nail exploded into the air, just missing Bradley's face and ricocheting across the kitchen floor. "Dagnabbit!"

Stanley yelled, popping his finger in his mouth. Then he turned and looked down at Bradley. "Go ahead, say it," he growled. "Not like I wouldn't have if the tables had been turned."

Bradley smiled and shook his head. "I don't need to say a thing," he said. "Just as long as we both know what I would have said."

Just then the front door opened, and Margaret and Timothy, Mary's parents, walked in. "Where can I put these things down?" Timothy asked, his arms filled with packages. "I think my darling here packed everything but the kitchen sink."

"Over here," Rosie called. "There's plenty of room on the kitchen counter."

Timothy hurried past Bradley and Stanley to place the packages where Rosie had suggested, and then he turned to the two men to see what they were doing. "Well, you aren't going to get nails through that wall," he said.

"What? Why?" Bradley asked.

"Well, that wall was originally the outside wall before the previous owners added the new dining room and kitchen," he said. "That's concrete underneath that plasterboard."

Bradley turned to Stanley. "Um, yeah, we knew that," Bradley said. "Right, Stanley?"

"Of course we knew that," Stanley said. "We ain't no fools."

"So, Timothy, just to be polite, what would you suggest we do?" Bradley asked. "We have to hang this curtain so Mary doesn't see what's behind it."

Timothy slowly looked around the room. "Well, if it were me," he said, "I'd string a length of clothesline from that kitchen cabinet over there," he pointed to the cabinet at the far end of the kitchen, "to that curtain rod over there." He pointed to a curtain rod in the far corner of the dining room. "Then I'd use clothespins to attach the sheets."

"That's brilliant," Bradley said. "I just have to run to the hardware store and get clothesline and clothespins."

"But we don't have enough time," Rosie cried. "Kate and Mary will be back with the girls in less than an hour. Oh, she's going to see everything."

"I've an idea," Margaret said. "But it means that Mary might be even a little later getting home."

"That would actually be a wonderful idea," Bradley said. "I haven't even begun to decorate the front porch yet."

"Well, why don't I go over to the school and volunteer to take the girls trick-or-treating with Kate so Mary can get back to the office, put her feet up for

245

a bit and finish up on any paperwork or calls she might have?" Margaret suggested.

"Oh, Margaret, that would be perfect," Rosie said.

"And then you, my dear," Margaret said to Timothy, "can give Bradley a hand here."

Timothy nodded. "I'll drop Margaret off at the school and then run to the hardware store," he said. "I'll be back as quick as a flash, so you can start on your porch decorations right away."

"Really?" Bradley asked, excitement glowing in his eyes.

"Aye, but I get to help once I'm home," he stipulated.

"Of course," Bradley said. "I have a feeling I'm going to need you."

"Then it's a deal," Timothy said. "Come along, Margaret my love, let's be on our way."

Chapter Forty-seven

The parade lasted thirty-five minutes as the little ghosts, ghouls and princesses made their way around the school several times so neighbors and relatives could take photos. "Why do I always forget my camera on days like today?" Mary muttered.

"Um, you have a smart phone in your pocket," Mike said as he appeared next to her. "It has a camera."

She smiled at him and then quickly looked around to see if anyone noticed her smiling at an empty space. No one noticed as far as she could see. "Thanks," she whispered. "You're a genius."

She reached into the pocket of the gypsy skirt and pulled out her phone. Swiping on the camera icon, the screen opened up, and she focused on Clarissa and Maggie, smiling at the crowd and waving their hands like the princesses they were. "Perfect," Mary said, taking a few more shots just to be sure.

"So, how did you like the presentation?" he asked.

"It was amazing," she replied softly. "I couldn't believe it when Abraham Lincoln came strolling into the classroom. I have never been so star-struck before in my life."

"Did you tell him how the play ended?" Mike asked.

"What?" Mary asked, forgetting to keep her voice soft and getting strange glances from the people around her. She quickly held her phone up to her ear. "Sorry, I guess my speaker wasn't working. Is this better?"

She smiled at the people around her who nodded in understanding. Then, keeping her phone to her ear, she turned back to Mike. "That wasn't funny," she said.

"Oh, I wasn't trying to be funny," he said, trying to keep a straight face. "I just figured maybe his unfinished business had something to do with not seeing the end. It would bug me forever if I had to walk out before the end of a movie."

She stared at him. "You know, for an angel, you have an awfully weird sense of humor," she said.

He grinned. "Yeah, I know." He paused and looked around at the children, his eyes resting on Clarissa and Maggie as they laughed together. "You're doing a good job, Mary," he said. "Never doubt that."

"Thanks, Mike," she replied. "After her teacher suggesting that I'm raising Wednesday

248

Adams, it's nice to hear some positive reinforcement."

He laughed. "If her teacher only knew," he said.

Mary chuckled, too. "I think she'd be a little shocked."

"So the reason I stopped by, other than to check out the parade, was to let you know that your parents have arrived in town," he said. "They're on their way here, to the school."

Mary looked around, still keeping her phone to her ear. "Oh, really?" she asked. "Where are they?"

Suddenly her phone started to ring, and the people around her looked confused. She smiled brightly and moved away from the crowd. "Hello?" she answered.

"Mary-Mary," her father's voice boomed over the phone. "We're here at Clarissa's school, but there are a lot of other people here, too. Where can we find you?"

"Well, the parade is ending, and we're going to be bringing the kids back to the classrooms now," she explained. "But if you go to the front door and down to the office, they'll give you a pass to the classroom. Just let them know you're Clarissa's grandparents."

"We'll do that," Timothy said. "See you in a couple of minutes, darling."

Mary helped herd the children back into the classroom, and then she and Kate passed out the treat bags to each student. The teacher played a CD of Halloween songs, and the children were allowed to visit with each other while the adults put the room back in order. Mary's parents joined them and pitched in.

"I'm glad Halloween only happens once a year," Mrs. Spangler said. "It's more exhausting than Christmas."

A few minutes before the children were to be dismissed, the volunteers went to the back of the room to relax for a few moments. Mary slouched into a metal folding chair, stretching her feet out in front of her.

"Mary, you look tired," Margaret said.

"Well, my feet are a little sore," she admitted. "But I'm so glad I came. I had a great time."

"Well, I have a suggestion for you," Margaret said. "And Bradley seconded it."

"Oh?" Mary said, sitting up. "What's that?"

"Well, I volunteered to go trick-or-treating with Clarissa, and your da volunteered to help Bradley put the front porch in order," she said. "So, you can go back to your office for a couple of hours, wrap up anything you need to and then come back to the house for dinner."

"Oh, I couldn't let you do that," Mary said.

"Darling, you wouldn't make it down the first block of trick-or-treating, the way you look," she said. "Besides, Kate will show me the ropes, won't you Kate?"

"Certainly," Kate said. "Besides, the girls had already planned to go together."

"But, I should…" Mary started.

"You should be at your office with the shades pulled down, your feet up on your desk and soft music playing," her mother insisted. "And you should try to relax, because, heaven knows, once your brothers get here, there will be no relaxing for you."

Mary paused. Going back to her office and just relaxing sounded wonderful. Besides, she justified, she could file away all the papers from the Kristen Banks case. She looked up and smiled at her parents and Kate. "I would love to do that," she said.

"Well, good," Margaret said.

"I'll just drive home and change first," Mary said.

"No!" Margaret cried, and then she clapped her hand over her mouth. "I mean, darling, once you go home, you know there's no way you'll get back out. Bradley will have you helping him decorate the front porch in no time."

"But look what I'm wearing," Mary said.

"It's Halloween," Kate inserted. "All of the owners of the stores in downtown Freeport are dressed up for Halloween today. You'll fit right in."

Mary sighed. "You're right," she said. "Okay, I'm going to escape for a few hours. And I'll try not to feel too guilty."

Margaret laughed. "Oh, yes, do feel guilty about allowing me to take my granddaughter trick-or-treating," she said. "Go, relax. You deserve a little downtime."

Chapter Forty-eight

Mary opened a mini-box of chocolate-covered caramels and popped one into her mouth as she entered her office.

"Are you really sure you should be eating those?"

Mary froze and turned to find Kristen sitting at her desk and Andrew standing behind her.

"What?" Mary asked. "What are you doing here?"

"See, that's the problem," Kristen said. "We don't know, and we figured you were supposed to know. But if you don't know, we're all screwed."

Shaking her head, Mary closed the blinds at the front of her office and walked over to her chair. "Sorry, but if I'm going to figure this out, I'm going to have to sit down," she said.

"Fine," Kristen said, getting out of the chair.

Andrew glided over next to Mary and leaned down near her. "Um, Mary," Andrew stuttered, "Mary, I can see Miss Banks now, and she doesn't look all that great."

"I can hear you," Kristen said, turning to Andrew with her hands on her hips. "And quite frankly, you don't look too hot yourself."

"You two can see each other?" Mary asked, looking from one ghost to the other.

"Duh," Kristen said. "We've got this whole weird, dead alumni thing going on."

"But Mitch confessed," Mary said. "You both should be ready to move on."

Kristen glided next to Andrew and shook her head. "Mitch did it?" Kristen asked. "It really doesn't seem like something Mitch would do."

Mary shrugged. "Well, he confessed, and he was pretty aggressive when Bradley and I were going back into the school to find Andrew."

"That's it? That's all you have?" Kristen asked, her eyebrows raised in surprise.

"Well, you know, once someone confesses, you kind of stop looking for more clues," Mary replied, feeling a little defensive.

"Well, something's going on," Kristen said. "Because I think if this is resolved, I shouldn't be here anymore."

"Maybe it's something between the two of you," Mary suggested. "Maybe Andrew needed to

254

say goodbye to you or thank you for being the motivation in his life."

Andrew shrugged. "Or the reason I got murdered," he said, folding his arms over his chest and turning away from Kristen.

"Hey, listen, I didn't ask you to investigate my death," she replied, poking him in his shoulder.

He spun around and faced her. "But you said you believed in me," he argued. "How could I not try to find out the truth? It was like a message from the grave."

She sighed. "Well, when I was writing it, I didn't mean it to be life-changing," she said. "I just wanted you to apply yourself to your spelling words. That's all. I didn't know I was going to die."

The anger left his face, and he nodded. "It was life-changing," Andrew admitted. "So, thank you for that. I accomplished a lot of things I never would have without that note. It meant a lot."

Kristen smiled at him. "You're welcome," she said. "You were my favorite in that class."

"Really?" he asked with a wide smile.

"Yeah, really," she said, pausing for a moment and then turning to Mary. "Okay, we've done the nicey, nicey. Can we move on now?"

Mary looked around and waited for a few moments. "No, it doesn't look like it's happening," she said. "There has to be something else."

Mary picked up the file that held all of the information about the case. She put the journal to the side and started sorting through the letters. "So, you got letters from Danny and Mitch," Mary said.

"And Vic," Kristen said. "Let's not forget Vic."

"Yeah," Mary said, picking up the report Bradley brought about Mitch's service. "But Vic died in Vietnam."

"What? Vic didn't die," Kristen said.

"Yes, he did," Mary said, picking up the report. "He died saving Mitch's life."

"But, that's impossible. I got a letter from Vic the same day I got my last letter from Danny," she said.

Mary shook her head. "Well, it must have been delayed," Mary said, "because the report said that Mitch was at the hospital in Germany for six weeks before he was transferred home two weeks before you died. So, Vic had been dead for almost two months when you got that letter."

"Find the letter," Kristen said.

Mary sorted quickly and then found the one from Vic. She opened it and gasped softly. "It's dated on the inside," Mary said, "only two weeks earlier than the postmark date."

"So, is Vic still alive?" Kristen asked. "Has he been alive all this time?"

"This doesn't make any sense," Mary said, sorting through the letters for more correspondence from Vic.

Finding a dozen more letters, Mary laid them out on the table next to each other and compared them. "The handwriting is very similar in all of them," she said, slowly shaking her head. She looked up at Kristen and Andrew. "I'm not sure where all of this is going to lead, but it looks like there's a good reason for both of you to still be here."

She pulled her phone out of her pocket. "I'm going to call Bradley and let him know what I've found."

Chapter Forty-nine

The sound effect machine was turned up to full volume as Bradley, Stanley, Timothy and Clifford worked on the Halloween display on the front porch. The life-sized coffin was on one side of the porch with its animatronics plugged into an extension cord that ran under the porch and into the basement. The speaker system was currently being attached to the rafters of the porch.

"Okay, try it again," Bradley called down from the top of the ladder.

Timothy walked past the coffin and tripped the sensor. Suddenly, the coffin lid started to lift, and a skeletal hand began to slip out of the darkness toward the unsuspecting trick-or-treater. "Good evening," the voice from inside the coffin called out.

"I think you need a little more bass on the voice," Clifford called, adjusting the sound through his tablet. "Yeah, this is going to be great."

Bradley's cell phone was in the pocket of his jacket that was currently hanging over a witch's brewing pot on the other side of the porch. It rang and rang, the tone drowned out by the sound effects all around them.

"This is awesome," Bradley called. "Just a couple more tries, and then we can hang up the screaming banshee."

"I almost got the lights working," Stanley called from the yard in front of the porch. He plugged a thick cord into a power strip that also held the sound and the animatronics. Suddenly, there was a loud pop, and everything went dark and quiet.

"Dagnabbit," Stanley cursed. "That's what you get fer buying cheap power strips."

"Or that's what you get for overloading a circuit," Bradley said. "Stanley, unplug the lights, and I'll go down to the basement and flip the fuse back on. And, I'll bring you your very own extension cord."

He closed the door just as his cell starting ringing again.

"Hey, Timothy," Clifford yelled. "Do you want to grab Bradley's cell phone?"

Timothy started across the porch but halted when the phone stopped ringing. "Oh well, if it was important, they'll call back," he said.

Mary hung up the phone and exhaled loudly. "He's not answering, and I already left him a message," she said to Kristen and Andrew. "So, the next best thing is to go home and talk to him in person."

259

"Shouldn't you call the police?" Andrew asked. "Let them know?"

"I don't know what I'd tell them," she said. "All I have is a forty-year-old letter that really could have been sent by another soldier who found it in Vic's belongings and decided to forward it on." She sighed in frustration. "We know that things aren't as wrapped up as the police believe, because the two of you haven't crossed over yet. But, they tend not to believe in paranormal evidence."

Kristen glided to the front of the office and stared at the window. Then she turned around and looked at Mary. "You need to be careful, Mary," she said. "You need to worry about you and your baby before you concern yourself with Andrew and me."

Andrew nodded. "Yeah, we don't want you to get hurt."

Kristen looked over at Andrew. "Hurt? This guy plays for keeps. Mary, we don't want you to be killed."

"I don't plan on getting myself killed," Mary said. "But I'd appreciate it if you two stayed close tonight so all of us can keep an eye on things."

"No problem," Andrew said.

"Yeah, we know how well that worked the last time there was danger," Kristen said to him. "You ran away."

"Actually, Kristen, I asked him to leave," Mary said. "Andrew didn't know he was dead yet. So without a body holding him back, once he thought about leaving, he just went to the place he was thinking about."

"Yeah, I wouldn't have deserted Mary. I promise," Andrew said. "I just was gone."

"Well, don't just *go* this time," Kristen said. "We need to all work together to keep Mary safe and to find out who killed us."

Mary packed up the journal, letters and everything else from the case and put them in her briefcase. She slipped her phone back in her pocket and then went to the door. The sun had gone down, and the street lights were glowing down over the scarecrows. Her car was only a few yards away, but suddenly her heart seemed to catch in her throat.

"Wait!" Kristen called out before Mary could open the door. "Let me check and make sure it's clear."

Kristen slipped through the wall, and then both Mary and Andrew heard her gasp in shock.

"What?" Mary asked as Kristen slipped back inside. "What's out there?"

"It's disgusting. Some of the things women were wearing," Kristen said, her face screwed up in disgust. "Don't people have mirrors? Don't they look in them before they leave their homes?"

Mary sighed. "Kristen, was there anything threatening outside?" she asked.

"Only if you count the threat to good taste," Kristen sniffed.

"Okay, then," Mary said. "I'm going out to my car. I'll meet both of you back at my house."

Chapter Fifty

"Mary just pulled up," Rosie called from the front room back into the kitchen.

"What? She wasn't supposed to be here for another hour," Bradley exclaimed. "Okay everyone, back here behind the curtains."

Suddenly, they heard a pop, and all of the lights on the ground floor shut off. "Dagnabbit," Stanley said back behind the curtain. "How's a man to know that outlets in the kitchen and the porch are connected?"

Bradley sighed. "Don't worry," he said. "I'll take care of it."

"But what are we going to do?" Timothy asked. "With no lights on, how are we going to surprise her?"

Bradley looked around the room frantically until he spied the bags of candy for the trick-or-treaters. "Margaret, Mary expects you and Timothy to be here, so would you ask her to fill up all the candy bowls? By that time, I'll be back upstairs, and the lights will be on."

Margaret laughed. "I'll be happy to get rid of my daughter," she teased. "Now hurry and get the lights back on."

Bradley had barely dived beyond the curtains when Mary entered the front door. With just the light from the stairs on, she saw Clarissa and her parents in the room. "Hi," she said. "Where's Bradley?"

"Oh, he had to run downstairs to flip the breaker," her mother explained. "He'll be back in a moment."

"Well, I really need to speak with him," she said, walking towards the kitchen.

"No," Timothy said, taking his daughter's arm. "That's his surprise. You don't want to ruin it, do you?"

"Well, this is pretty important," she said.

"But, it can wait for just a few minutes, can't it?" her mother asked. "Besides, Bradley wanted you to fill the candy dishes out on the porch when you came home."

"What?" Mary asked.

Clarissa came over with four large bags of candy and handed them to her mother. "Daddy said it was really important that you do it right away," she insisted.

Mary shook her head. "But, I really do need to speak with Bradley."

"Darling," her father said, "fill the candy dishes, and we'll send Bradley out there in a trice. You don't want angry trick-or-treaters now, do you?"

"But…" she tried to argue.

"Go, darling," her father insisted, guiding her to the door. "There's nothing that important that it can't wait a moment."

Shaking her head, Mary closed the door behind her and walked down the steps to the sidewalk where a large bowl of candy sat on a chair. Since there was no light from the front porch, the bowl was in complete darkness. She could make out the shadow but had to feel around to be sure. "This is ridiculous," she muttered.

She began to open the first bag when she felt a pinprick in her side. She started to turn towards the pain when a strong hand reached out and grabbed her arm. "If you don't want your baby to die," the low voice threatened, "you'll do exactly what I say."

Mary gasped softly when she saw the glimmer of a knife up against the side of her stomach. She dropped the candy on the ground and nodded. "I'll do whatever you want," she said. "Just don't hurt my baby."

"Walk with me," the low voice said, "and don't make any stupid moves."

She was pushed forward onto the sidewalk and then guided down the block. She looked around at all of her neighbors and their children, dressed in costume and running from house to house. She knew any word from her would risk their safety. Then she glanced at the person next to her, and her heart stopped. A soldier dressed in camouflage with black face paint smeared over his face was her abductor.

"Where are you taking me?" she whispered.

The knife pressed a little tighter against her, and she felt it scratch her skin. She was suddenly shoved off the sidewalk and stumbled against the side of a dark SUV. The soldier reached out, opened the back door and pushed Mary into the back seat. "Turn with your hands behind your back."

Mary slid sideways on the seat and did as she was asked. She felt the coarse rope tighten against her wrist, and then she was forcefully shoved back against the seat. The solider reached over to grab the seatbelt just as another car turned the corner and light flooded into the back seat. With a jolt, Mary recognized her captor. She took a deep breath and waited until the soldier had climbed into the front seat and turned on the ignition.

"Where are you taking me?" she asked again.

"Someplace we can have some privacy," Viv replied. "Someplace in the jungle."

Chapter Fifty-one

"How long does it take to fill a bowl of candy?" Stanley muttered. "She don't have to arrange it pretty-like."

Rosie giggled. "Why of course she would want it to look nice, and maybe she's visiting with some of the neighbors," she whispered back to Stanley. "She'll be in any moment."

Bradley tapped his fingers impatiently and then shook his head. "This is taking too long. It's been nearly ten minutes," he said, and he hurried to the front door and pulled it open. The lights were now on, and he could clearly see the chair and the bags of candy dropped by the side. His stomach dropped.

"Mary!" he yelled, walking to the edge of the porch and scanning up and down the sidewalk. "Mary!"

He ran down the stairs and up to the sidewalk. "Mary!" he yelled. "Mary!"

"Bradley what's wrong?" Margaret asked, standing in the doorway.

"Mary's gone," Bradley said.

"She said she needed to talk to you," Timothy said, his voice filled with self-recrimination. "As soon as she came into the house, she said she needed to talk to you. And I told her it could wait."

"Okay, we need search the neighborhood," Sean O'Reilly said as he walked onto the porch and was joined by his two brothers, Art and Tom. "She can't have gone too far. Everyone have their cell phones?"

Bradley reached to his back pocket and shook his head. "My cell phone," he said.

He ran back up the stairs and into the house, grabbing his jacket that he'd thrown over the couch. Pulling the phone out of the pocket, he looked at the screen. "She tried to call me twice," he said, clicking on the message.

He listened to the message and turned to Mary's brothers. "I think she's been taken," he said.

Maggie, standing in the corner of the room, tugged on Clarissa's arm. But Clarissa, concentrating on her father, ignored her. Maggie tugged on her arm again. "What?" Clarissa asked impatiently.

"There are some ghosts in your house," Maggie said. "And they're trying to talk to your dad."

Clarissa grabbed Maggie's hand. "Where?"

Clarissa gasped. The two ghosts stood next to Bradley. One was a woman with her head partially bashed in and blood covering her face, and the other was a man with a pale face and blood covering his clothes. "Mary!" the woman was shouting. "Mary!"

Clarissa pulled Maggie across the room with her. "What?" she asked. "What did you say about my mom?"

Bradley turned to Clarissa. "Clarissa?"

"There are ghosts here," Maggie said to Bradley. "And they know about Mary."

Kristen turned to Maggie. "We saw a soldier take her," she said. "Tell your dad a soldier has her, and he told her he was taking her to a jungle."

"They said the soldier has her," Clarissa said. "They said the soldier is taking her to the jungle."

"A jungle?" Bradley asked. "What jungle?"

"How the hell am I supposed to know?" Kristen huffed. "I'm not from Freeport. Where do you have jungles in Freeport?"

"She's not from Freeport," Clarissa said. "She doesn't know."

"The woods," Andrew suggested. "He's taking her to the woods."

"The other one said he's taking her to the woods," Clarissa repeated.

Bradley looked around the room. "Our best guess is that she's being taken to a woods, either Krape Park or Oakdale," he said. "Probably in a heavily wooded section."

"He has a knife," Clarissa said, her eyes filling with tears. "He has a knife on mommy."

Kristen punched Andrew. "You didn't need to tell that little girl about the knife," she said.

"Yes, I did," Andrew argued. "That's how he killed me, and it's how he'll try and kill her."

"Okay," Sean said. "How do you want us to do this?"

"We've got at least two highly likely places," Bradley said, "one on the south side of town at Oakdale and the other one in Krape Park, following the road up to Flagstaff. I want at least two cars going to Krape Park and two to Oakdale. No loud noises. We don't want to panic this guy."

He turned to Sean. "You take Krape Park," he said. "Call me if you see anything."

"Got it," Sean called. "Art, you can come with me, we'll take the front."

Timothy threw Tom his keys. "You drive," he said. "We'll follow Sean."

270

"I'm going," Clifford said, standing up and pulling his keys out of his pocket. "Stanley, you can come with me. We'll go the back way to Oakdale."

"Okay, I'll see you there," Bradley said.

Bradley was running towards his car when Ian stepped out of his car.

"Hey, I thought the party was inside," he said.

"No time to explain," Bradley called to him. "Jump in the cruiser with me."

Running to his car, Bradley quickly turned it on and shoved it into drive. He waited only a moment for Ian to get in, and then he pulled down the street towards Highway 26.

"Mike!" he yelled, and Mike appeared next to him.

"Go to her," Bradley said. "Be with her."

"On my way," Mike replied and faded out.

Chapter Fifty-two

Mary stared into the rearview mirror and looked at the driver. Beneath the smeared, black paint, she could see the familiar features of the friendly waitress who had helped them the other day. But her eyes were now slightly dilated, and her jaw was clenched tightly. She looked like someone who was in a trance.

"Viv?" Mary asked.

"I'm not Viv," she barked out, her face emotionless and her voice several octaves lower than Mary had remembered. "I'm Private Victor Kutchens. My family calls me Vic."

Is she just playing a game, or does she really think she's her dead brother? Mary wondered.

A movement in the passenger's seat across from Viv caught Mary's eye, and she turned to see the ghost of a young man appear. He was clothed in a military dress uniform, and he bore a striking resemblance to the woman driving the SUV.

"The real Vic?" Mary whispered.

The young soldier turned to Mary and nodded. "I've been trying to help her for years. It's like she goes away and this other person comes out. This person isn't like me at all," he said. "But she doesn't realize when he takes over. It's like she goes to sleep, and he comes out."

Mary had read that multiple personalities can be caused by trauma, and it sure sounded like Viv had had plenty of trauma in her life. But, whoever the bad Vic was, he obviously thought Mary was a threat and needed to be eliminated. Her only hope was to try and get in touch with Viv.

"I think I met your sister, Viv," Mary said. "Doesn't she own a diner in Polo?"

"She bought that diner with blood money," Viv snapped.

Mary was struck by the anger in Viv's voice. Did she have so much guilt about buying the diner that she hated herself?

"I'd think, as her brother, you'd be more understanding," Mary replied. "I mean, she lost everyone in her life. What else could she do?"

"She could have died with me," she growled. "She could have laid down her life and died with me."

"I never felt that way," the real Vic said. "I was grateful she had money to start a new life."

Mary nodded sympathetically at Vic.

"You wanted her to lay down her life, like you laid down your life for Mitch?" Mary asked Viv.

273

Viv clenched her jaw again and shook her head. "No, what I did was valiant," he said. "All Viv did was take what she wanted. She was selfish."

"In a way," Mary said. "But in a way some could say that you were selfish when you chose to risk your life and leave your sister all alone."

Viv swerved the SUV to the curb and turned in the seat. "Do you want to die right now?" she screamed. "Do you want me to kill you right now?"

She grabbed the knife and held it at Mary's throat. "I can do it," she threatened. "I've done it before."

Mary leaned back as far as she could, her heart hammering against her chest. "No," she stammered. "I'm sorry."

Viv turned back in her seat and pulled back onto the road. "I did what every soldier should do," she said. "I sacrificed for my country."

"And Viv did what every survivor has to do," Mary replied. "She tried to move on with her life. But it looks like you didn't let her move on."

Viv shook her head. "No, it's not like that," she said, shaking her head. "You're confusing things." Her voice got frantic. "Just shut up and let me drive."

"I'm sorry," Vic said. "I've tried to reach her. Tried to reach her when she went after that poor young man. I've tried to reach her since the accident with Kristen, but, she can't or won't hear me."

Mary nodded, still trying to calm down. How long had she been gone from the house? Fifteen minutes? She knew that they'd eventually figure out she was missing, but would it be soon enough? Suddenly, she felt the hairs on the back of her neck stand up. She turned and saw Mike sitting next to her. Tears of relief filled her eyes and slid down her cheeks.

"Hey, sweetheart," he said gently. "How are you doing?"

When he saw her hands were tied, he gently wiped away her tears. "Don't worry; the cavalry is on its way. And I'll be here for moral support."

Viv turned left on Lamm Road, and Mary realized they'd be at Oakdale in a few short minutes. She had to buy herself some time.

"I have a question before we get to the jungle," Mary said. "What turned you from a hero into a killer?"

The SUV screeched to a halt, sliding up against the edge of the road. Viv turned around again, her face twisted. "I am not a killer!" she screamed. "I'm a hero! I protect people. I help people. I'm not a killer."

275

"So, Kristen Banks," Mary said, trying to keep her voice calm. "Did you kill her?"

"No!" Viv screamed. "I loved her. I loved her, but she wouldn't even acknowledge me. So, I went to her and tried to get her to see reason. But then..."

Viv shook her head. "I don't know. It all happened so fast," she said. "I was holding her, and then she was falling. I didn't push her. I didn't mean to push her. I loved her."

"Why did you go to the school?" Mary asked.

"I had to see her," Viv answered. "I knew Danny was coming home, and I had to get her to change her mind."

"How did you know about Danny?"

"His mother came by the diner," Viv said. "She told me."

"Did she tell Viv?" Mary asked.

"No, no I was at the diner," Viv said. "It was me, not Viv."

"But I thought Viv bought the diner with blood money," Mary pushed. "How could you be there? Weren't you dead?"

"I'm not dead!" Viv screamed, pounding her fist on the steering wheel. "I'm here!"

"Okay, I was just a little confused," Mary replied softly. "So you found out that Danny was coming home, and you wanted to see Kristen and get her to change her mind."

"I was much better for her than Danny would ever be," Viv said. "I was a better man all around."

"I read the letters you sent her," Mary said, "when you were overseas. I could tell you cared for her, but it seemed to me the letters were written more to a friend than a lover."

"What?" Viv asked, looking at Mary through the rearview mirror.

"The letters didn't change until after you died," Mary said. "And then, suddenly, they were filled with expressions of love and passion. It was strange. Why would you change like that?"

"I loved Kristen," Viv said. "I know I did."

The SUV pulled back onto the road, and they continued in silence for a few minutes. Finally, Viv turned down Baileyville Road towards Oakdale. Mary knew she only had a short amount of time before they were hidden in the woods.

"I've been thinking about those letters," she said. "And the more I think about it, the more I realize the letters were from a friend to a friend," Mary said. "As a matter of fact, the letters were more

277

about Mitch than anything else. It was like the two of you had a mutual admiration society…"

Mary stopped and realized what she was saying. "Mitch," she said slowly with dawning realization. "Vic didn't love Kristen, he loved Mitch."

Vic turned in his seat and nodded at Mary. "Yes, you're right," he said. "And now you figured out my greatest secret."

Chapter Fifty-three

"Okay, I'm in, now what's going on?" Ian asked as they moved through the residential streets toward Highway 26.

"Mary's been taken," Bradley said. "We were working on a case, and we thought it was safe."

"She's been taken?" Ian repeated. "How long?"

"Fifteen to twenty minutes ago," Bradley said. "But the guy's already murdered twice."

"Are the two ghosts in the back of your car the victims?" Ian asked, looking over his shoulder to see Kristen and Andrew behind him.

"Does everyone you know see ghosts?" Kristen asked Bradley.

"Ah, well darling, he can't hear you without Mary around," Ian said. "But if you could fill me in on any details, that would be helpful."

"He said the jungle," Andrew inserted, "but it looks like he's taking her to Oakdale."

"But it's not he. It's she," Kristen said. "It's not Vic, it's Viv."

Ian turned to Bradley. "I don't know if this is going to make sense," he said. "But he is not a he, he's a she. It's Viv not Vic. And she's taking Mary to Oakdale."

"What the hell?" Bradley asked, turning on the sirens once they got on to Highway 26 and headed out of town. He punched on his radio. "Connect me with the Polo Police Department," he said. "I want to have a detective in the room with detainee Mitch Howse so I can ask him some questions concerning a crime in progress."

They waited in tense silence for several minutes before they were connected to a speaker phone. "Okay, Chief Alden, we have him here," the voice on the other end said.

"Howse, Viv Kutchens has kidnapped Mary O'Reilly," he said. "Viv's dressed as a soldier and has Mary at knifepoint. We are heading to intercept her, so if there is anything you can do to give us insight and maybe save Viv's life, I would suggest you start talking right away."

"She thinks she's Vic," Mitch said into the phone. "It started after she learned that Vic had been killed in action. She'd appear at my house, dressed like Vic, talking like Vic, and she'd visit with me for a couple of hours. But she'd never remember anything about it later."

"Sounds like dissociative identity disorder," Ian said. "They used to call it split personalities, but now they understand more about it."

"When she was Vic she was pretty hard on Viv, blamed Viv for everything," Mitch continued. "I was always arguing on Viv's behalf. Then, one day she came to the house. She had blood on her clothes, and she told me that Kristen Banks was dead."

There was silence on the other end for a few moments. "It was an accident," Mitch said. "And what could I do? Vic was the one who was there at the school, but Viv would be the one who got punished."

"So, you covered it up," Bradley said.

"Yeah, there was nothing we could do about her death," Mitch said, "and everyone said it was an accident. So I just went along with things."

"Then what happened?" Bradley asked.

"After a while, Vic went away," Mitch said. "And Viv seemed to be leading a happy, normal life. But then, a couple of weeks ago, Vic showed up at my house again. He was dressed in old Army fatigues, and he was upset because someone was looking into Kristen's death."

"About the time Andrew started looking into it," Bradley surmised.

"Vic was talking about protecting Viv," Mitch said. "And I tried to tell him that I'd take care of her, but he kept going on about making sure nothing happened to Viv. I tried to keep everyone away from the school, but somehow…"

"Vic killed again," Bradley said.

"She's sick," Mitch pleaded. "She's real sick. Please don't shoot her."

"I'm not promising anything," Bradley said. "She's got my wife. But I'll do my best to bring her back and get her the help she needs."

Chapter Fifty-four

Viv pulled the SUV into the dark and deserted parking lot of Oakdale Nature Preserves and followed the tree-lined path back behind the old dormitories into the woods. Mary took an unsteady breath. This was not a good place to be.

"It's going to be okay," Mike said. "We've been in tougher fixes than this."

"Yes," Mary whispered. "But this time, I don't know if I can get through to her."

"Who are you talking to?" Viv asked.

"The reason Andrew asked me to help him find out the truth behind Kristen's death was because I can see and communicate with ghosts," Mary said to Viv. "I don't know if you'll believe me, but the ghost of Vic is sitting next to you in your car."

Viv shook her head and blinked rapidly. "No, that's impossible," she said. "I'm Vic. I didn't die."

"Well, okay," Mary said. "He must be an imposter. But he sure looks like Vic. Is there anything I can ask him to prove he's not who he says he is?"

Viv jumped out of the car and came around to the back seat. She opened the door, grabbed the rope around Mary's hands and pulled her backwards. Mary tripped out of the car and landed hard on the leaf-covered ground.

"You think you're so smart, just like those psychologists they used to send us to when we were kids. Well, I don't believe you," Viv said, brandishing her knife. "And now you are going to die."

"Listen to yourself, Viv. You sound like Mom," Vic cried. "You sound like Mom when she was crazy."

Mary took a shaky breath. "He just said you sound like your mom," she repeated. "When she was crazy."

Viv's breath was labored, coming out in gasping sobs. "No," she said. "It's a trick."

"Remember how you used to hide me when Mom was on the war path?" he asked. "She'd beat you, but you'd never tell."

"You'd let your mom beat you," Mary said,. "so Vic would be safe."

Viv lifted the knife over her head. "No, I don't believe it!" she screamed. "You're lying. You're all lying. And now you're going to die."

Mary rolled onto her back and kicked Viv in the stomach with all of her might, connecting and sending her rolling backwards down the embankment.

"Get up," Mike called, standing next to her. "She's coming back."

Mary rolled onto her side and struggled to get into a sitting position without the use of her hands. It just wasn't working. "I can't," she breathed. "I can't get up."

"You bitch!" Viv screamed, grabbing small tree trunks and pulling herself up the embankment. "You can't escape me."

"Remember when you killed mom?" Vic screamed. "Remember when we promised we'd never tell anyone else. You did it to save my life."

"You killed your mother to save Vic's life," Mary breathed. "You saved him."

Reaching the top of the embankment, her knife clutched in her fist, Viv froze. "How did you know that?" she asked Mary.

"Vic told me," Mary pleaded. "He's here. He's been here all along, trying to help you."

"She found out about me," Vic said. "She was punching me and calling me a queer. She said she'd beat it out of me."

"He said that your mother was beating him because she found out he was gay," Mary repeated.

285

Shaking her head, Viv dropped to her knees. "I'm not gay," she cried roughly. "I'm straight, and I loved Kristen."

Vic walked over to his sister and knelt by her side. "I thought you understood," he said.

"He thought you understood," Mary said.

Viv ripped her hat off her head, allowing her hair to spill down. "Being gay is what killed him," she cried, sobbing harshly. Her voice sounded feminine again as she stammered her words. "He went on a suicide mission because of it. He gave his life for Mitch because he loved him."

"I loved Mitch," Vic said remorsefully, "but he didn't love me. We actually talked about it." He laughed sadly. "Mitch was pretty surprised to find out how I felt. But we were honest with each other. It's ironic really; the person he loved was the only other person I ever really loved. Mitch loved you."

Mary closed her eyes and drew in a deep breath. *Okay, that is not my story to tell,* she thought.

"Viv," she breathed. "Vic didn't commit suicide. He was a soldier, and he did what he thought was right. It had nothing to do with his sexual preferences and everything to do with him being brave and noble. Don't take that away from him."

Viv looked up. "I don't believe you," she said, her voice low and raspy once again. She picked up her hat and stuffed her hair back inside of it. "This is a trick, and you're lying to me. Vic isn't dead. I'm Vic."

Standing, she lifted her knife. "And now you're going to pay," she cried, dashing forward towards Mary.

Chapter Fifty-five

The crack of the bullet echoed in the woods, and the knife Viv was holding tore out of her hand and back into the underbrush. Then Bradley walked out of the woods, his gun drawn and pointed at Viv. "I want you to put your hands on your head and drop down to your knees," he ordered. "Now!"

"Who are you?" Viv screamed.

"I'm Master Sergeant Bradley Alden, 75th Regiment," Bradley said. "And Private, I need you to cooperate with me."

Viv immediately put her hands on her head and knelt down. "Sir. Yes, sir," she shouted back.

Bradley walked forward and quickly cuffed Viv's hands behind her back. He helped her stand and started to move her toward the road.

Thinking only Bradley had arrived, Mary was surprised when she felt a tug behind her as the ropes around her wrists fell away and then strong hands helped her to a sitting position. She turned around to find Ian squatting next to her. "Ian?" she said, "What are you doing here?"

He smiled at her and wrapped his arm around her waist to help her to her feet. "Well, darling, it's

Halloween," he said. "Where else would I be but with the O'Reillys?"

"Ian, would you mind?" Bradley asked, motioning to Viv.

Ian nodded towards Bradley and then looked at Mary. "Can you stand on your own, darling?" he asked. "I can promise you it'll only be for a wee moment."

"Yes," she said with a nod. "Yes, I can."

Hurrying over, Ian took possession of a handcuffed Viv and nodded. "I'll take her back towards the car," he said. "Give you two a moment."

Bradley hurried over and wrapped his arms around Mary, just holding her for a moment. "I'm so sorry I didn't answer my phone," he whispered. "I'm never going to forgive myself…"

She looked up at him, placed her fingers on his lips and met his eyes. "Good shooting, Tex," she said. "And good timing."

He pulled her tightly against him again. "Are you okay?" he asked. "Are you really okay?"

"I'm fine, only…" she paused.

"What is it sweetheart? Anything you want."

"Could you please help me find a restroom?" she asked. "It's been a really long night."

Chuckling, he guided her to the bathrooms that were located on the other side of the dormitory building. "One of my officers will pick Viv up, and then we'll go back home," he said.

"Oh, good," Mary said. "I am so looking forward to a little peace and quiet."

Chapter Fifty-six

Bradley helped Mary out of the car and, with his arm wrapped around her waist, guided her up the stairs into their home. "I can walk, really," she said to him.

"You're just lucky I'm not carrying you," he growled softly. "I don't think I'm ever going to let you out of my sight again."

"I really did try to contact you," she said.

"I know," he replied, kissing the side of her face. "I was distracted with too many things. But that will never happen again, I promise."

"Distracted?" she asked. "Distracted with what?"

Before he could answer, the front door of their house burst open, and a chorus of voices filled the yard. Mary looked around. Her entire family, the Brennan clan, Rosie and Stanley were all coming out to meet her. When Ian walked up from behind them and joined the group, she was nearly overwhelmed. She turned to Bradley in total confusion. "What?" she began.

"Happy Baby Shower," Bradley whispered.

"A baby shower?" she squeaked, tears filling her eyes.

"Kate and Rosie, along with your mom, have been planning it for weeks," he said. And then leaning closer, he whispered, "those witches."

"Oh," she said, clapping her hands over her mouth. "They were buying…"

"Baby shower stuff," he said. "Surprised?"

"To say the least," she replied, her voice thick with emotion. "Thank you."

An instant later she was caught up in a flurry of hugs and well wishes.

"Mary, my sweet girl, are you okay?" her mother asked.

"Fine, Ma, really," Mary said. "I'm more hungry than anything else."

"Well then, why didn't you say so?" her mother replied. "I'll run in and start making you a plate."

"My own Mary-Mary," Timothy said, wrapping her up in a big embrace. "Please forgive me for sending you out like that and not listening to you."

"Da, how were you to know that would happen?" she asked. "You were just trying to give me the surprise of my life. And I love you for it."

"I would have died twice over if anything had happened to you," he said.

"I'm fine, Da," she said. "Really."

Sean was the next one to greet her, shaking his head. "Always getting yourself in trouble," he said, giving her a gentle hug.

"Yeah, you should talk," she replied, returning the hug.

"We O'Reillys are sure badasses, aren't we?" he asked.

She chuckled. "Yes. Yes we are."

It took another ten minutes for everyone to wish her well and then be shooed back into the house for refreshments. Bradley walked with Mary up onto the porch and guided her to the swing at the far end. "I thought I'd give you a moment to catch your breath before you went in," he said.

She leaned back against the wooden slats and breathed in the cool autumn air. "Thank you," she said. "It's just what I needed."

The door creaked open, and Clarissa peeked her head out.

"Clarissa, sweetheart," Mary said, her arms outstretched. "Come and sit with us on the swing."

Clarissa ran across the porch and threw her arms around Mary. "I was so worried about you," she said. "Especially when Andrew told me the soldier had a knife."

"You spoke to Andrew?" Mary asked.

Clarissa nodded. "Maggie showed me how to see ghosts when I touch her," she said. "And when Maggie saw the ghosts at the house, I touched her hand, and then I talked to them."

"Clarissa and Maggie were the ones who told us who'd taken you," Bradley said. "They are the heroes tonight."

Mary laid her head on Clarissa's head. "Thank you so much," she said.

"The ghosts looked scary," Clarissa said. "Do they always look scary?"

"Not always," Mary said. "Especially…"

She paused as she looked over and saw Andrew and Kristen gliding onto the porch. "Bradley," Mary said. "Do you think you could sneak Maggie out here? There's something that I'd like the girls to see."

Within a few moments, Maggie and Bradley were out on the porch with Clarissa and Mary.

"Maggie, you and Clarissa hold hands," Mary said. "And Bradley, you hold on to me. Now, can you all see Kristen and Andrew?"

"What are we? Show and Tell?" Kristen asked.

"Well, actually, yes," Mary replied. "I hope you don't mind too much."

"But what are we supposed to do?" Andrew asked.

"You're supposed to go home," Mary replied "Because you've completed what you needed to down here, now you get to return to other side."

"But how?" Kristen asked.

"Just look around for a light," Mary said.

Suddenly, both Kristen and Andrew were engulfed with light, and the scary features from death that had marred their bodies slowly disappeared as they were made whole.

"I see the light," Andrew said with a wide smile. "Thank you, Mary."

He turned and started to walk away from them until his body faded from view.

"Thank you, Mary," Kristen said, and then she looked at Maggie and Clarissa. "And you two, you make sure you study hard so you can grow up to be whatever it is you want to be."

She looked up at Mary, tears in her eyes, and nodded. "Whatever you do, don't name your dog Kristen."

Mary laughed, tears in her voice. "I promise I won't," she said.

"And you," Kristen said finally, looking at Bradley. "Don't get fat."

Bradley nodded in her direction and smiled. "Thanks, I won't."

Kristen turned around and walked slowly away until she, too, faded into the light.

"That was the best thing ever," Clarissa said.

"Yes, it's pretty cool," Mary agreed.

"They're not scary when they're ready to go to heaven, are they?" Maggie said.

"No, they're not," Mary agreed. "They're all cleaned up and ready to go home."

Chapter Fifty-seven

Mary entered her home and nearly didn't recognize it. Blue balloons, streamers and confetti were everywhere. A beautiful floral arrangement with blue, white and yellow flowers stood in the middle of her table surrounded by an incredible amount of food. A large folding table was filled with packages wrapped in an assortment of blue wrapping paper, and next to the table stood an antique-looking rocking chair with a bright blue bow attached to it.

Mary's smile was a little watery as she looked around the room at her friends and family. "You'd think someone was having a baby boy," she teased as she wiped a few stray tears from her cheeks. "Thank you so much. I am completely overwhelmed."

"Well, sit yourself down so the party can begin," Stanley said. "That there rocking chair looks like the perfect place fer you to be."

"Stanley and Rosie's gift to you is the rocking chair," Bradley whispered.

Mary walked over and stroked the beautiful, golden oak chair with oak leaf and acorn carvings on the back and the sides. "This is just gorgeous," she said, turning and hugging Rosie and Stanley. "I have never seen anything so beautiful."

Stanley sniffled and smiled at Mary. "Well, try it on fer size, girlie," he said. "Take it out fer a spin."

Mary sat on the chair and relaxed. Pushing off, she rocked back and forth several times. "Oh, it's just perfect," she said.

Margaret appeared at her side carrying a plate of food. "Now that we finally have you sitting down," she said, "I thought I'd try and get some food inside of you."

Mary looked at the plate that was filled with a mini-sandwich, some vegetable sticks and dip, a little bit of fruit salad and three large slices of cheesecake. "What kind are these?" Mary asked, pointing her fork at the cheesecake.

"Pumpkin, salted caramel and dark chocolate," Margaret said. "Rosie made the pumpkin, I made the salted caramel, and Kate made the dark chocolate."

"You're joking!" Mary exclaimed, taking a forkful of the dark chocolate and closing her eyes in ecstasy as the flavors melted on her tongue. "This is amazing. Kate, I didn't know you knew how to make cheesecake."

"I didn't," Kate replied with a smile, "until Master Chef Rosie took me under her wing. Do you really like it?"

Mary put another forkful in her mouth. "Are you kidding me?" she said. "Um, these cheesecakes are all for the pregnant lady, right?"

She took a bite of each of the other cheesecakes and sighed happily. "I just love you guys," she said.

Margaret grinned. "Well, I knew what to put on her plate," she said. "She was always the one with the sweet tooth."

"But she needs to open the presents," Clarissa said.

"Of course I do," Mary replied and smiled gratefully at Bradley when he placed a TV tray next to the rocking chair for her plate. "Clarissa, could you bring the gifts to me?"

"Oh, and I'll write down who gave you what," Rosie said, holding up a pen and notepad.

"Thanks, Rosie," Mary replied.

She took the first gift from Clarissa, a large box that was fairly heavy.

"That's from our family," Maggie said.

Mary looked up and smiled. "Well then I can't wait to see what it is."

She opened the box, and once again, her eyes filled with tears as she pulled out a handmade baby

299

quilt in pastel blue colors. "Oh, it's beautiful," she said, and then she rubbed it against her cheek. "And so soft."

"We went with mom to the fabric store and made sure all the material was soft," Maggie said.

"And mom made all of us help quilt so it could be from the whole family," Andy said. "But she pretty much got all the blood stains out of it."

Mary chuckled and turned to Kate. "Thank you," she said, her heart in her eyes. "I truly love it."

Clarissa handed Mary the next box, a shirt-sized gift box. Mary opened the card and smiled up at Ian. "You know you didn't have to," she said.

"As an honorary uncle, it was both my duty and my pleasure," he replied.

She opened the box and started to laugh before she pulled out a tiny, baby-sized kilt, matching booties, and a tiny leather sporran.

"It's the MacDougal tartan, my family tartan," he explained.

"I love it," Mary said. "And I know he'll be proud to wear it."

The next box was from her brothers, and Mary opened it with a little bit of trepidation. But when she looked inside, she laughed again. First she pulled out a baby-sized Cubs baseball uniform, and then she pulled out a tiny Bears football jersey, a Bulls basketball onesie, and finally a Blackhawks hockey sleeper.

"Those are our family tartans," Sean said. "We need to start him early on the right teams to follow."

Mary handed them to Bradley. "What do you think?" she asked.

He was amazed at how tiny the sleeper was. "Will he fit in them?" he asked.

Nodding, Mary sighed. "They'll probably be too big at first."

"Now, it's time for your gift from Ma and me," Timothy said. He slipped into the kitchen and came back out carrying a wicker bassinet. "This is the bassinet you used when you were a baby," he said. "We've kept it up in the attic, waiting until the day you could use it for your own child."

His eyes filled with tears, and his voice cracked. He waited for a moment before he tried to speak. "I'm so proud of you," he said softly. "You've already become a wonderful mother. And I can't wait to meet little Timmy."

Margaret punched him softly on his arm. "That's Michael Timothy, you big galoot," she said, wiping tears from her own eyes.

"Ah, but he'll always be little Timmy to me," Timothy replied, winking at Mary.

Mary was just about to pick up her plate when the doorbell rang.

"I'll get it," Bradley said, and he hurried over to the door.

Because of the adventures earlier in the evening, everyone was quiet and tense, waiting to see who was at the door.

"Oh, I'm so sorry," a woman's voice floated into the room. "Are we too late? I didn't even know if we should have come."

"No, of course you should have come," Bradley said. "Please come in."

Bradley opened the door wide, and an older couple walked in carrying a large, wrapped box. The woman walked over to Mary. "I don't know if you remember me," she said. "We've only met a couple of times. I'm Mike's mother."

"Oh, good, they came," Margaret whispered to Rosie.

Unable to speak at first, with tears rolling down her cheeks, Mary nodded. "Yes, of course I remember you," she finally said. "Thank you so much for coming."

"It's all a little strange," Mike's mother said. "But somehow I had this strong impression that Mike would want you to have this."

Mike appeared next to her and smiled down at Mary. "She got the impression after I whispered it into her ear several dozen times," he said.

Mary took the gift and reverently unwrapped it. In the midst of fresh, light blue tissue paper lay a well-used baseball mitt and an autographed baseball. Mary lightly stroked the mitt, its leather worn and soft. "It's perfect," she said. "I know he will love it."

"They were my greatest treasures when I was a boy," Mike explained. "I wanted to pass them on."

"Do you really like it?" Mike's mother asked.

"Oh, I love it," Mary said.

Mike's mother turned to her husband, who'd come up behind her. "See, I told you she'd understand," she said.

He smiled down at Mary, looking so much like an older version of his son that her heart nearly broke. "Well, just in case, we brought you another gift, too," he said, handing her another box.

"Oh, you didn't need to," Mary said. "This is wonderful."

"Yeah, well, we thought he'd probably like this, too," he said.

Mary opened the box and pulled out a toy fire truck. "In case he ever wonders who he was named for," Mike's father said.

Bradley handed Mary a tissue to help stem the flow of tears, and she shook her head. "He will never wonder who he was named for," she promised. "He will always know."

Chapter Fifty-eight

The fire was glowing embers, and the house was dark, only the light from the jack-o-lantern glowing on the coffee table was softly illuminating the room. Mary was snuggled in Bradley's arms in the corner of the couch, and her father had moved the rocking chair to the center of the room where he now sat with Clarissa cuddled in his arms.

"We need one more story, Grandpa," Clarissa insisted.

"Ah, well then, who hasn't had a turn?" he asked, looking around the room at his family assembled around him.

"The only one who hasn't taken a turn is you," Margaret said. "So, make it a good one so we can all sleep with the covers pulled up tight."

Timothy chuckled. "And so I will," he said.

"The moon was full, as it is tonight, and a young girl was walking near the forest's edge all alone," he said, his voice low. "Now it wasn't her fault at all, for she was a good girl and abided her mother and father's warning, 'Never go near the dark woods at night.' But she'd been helping a friend, and it took much longer than she had expected. And now she walked slowly her heart hammering in her chest,

305

as the leaves crunched underneath her shoes and the wind cried softly between the trees."

"She clutched her shawl closer, for the night was a cold, autumn night, and the wind was fierce. The moonlight cast shadows through the trees that danced wickedly in the night sky, their spindly, leafless limbs lifted up reaching for the stars in the heavens. She'd heard about the trees and their autumnal dance but had never seen it before. It was almost as if they had lifted their roots from the ground and swayed to the music of the night, their giant trunks bending side to side and their silvered branches waving to the moon. The girl was awestruck by the beauty and the majesty of it. And that's where she made her first mistake. She stopped walking and turned toward the dark woods to watch."

"A light appeared in the woods a little ways from the road. A light that she wouldn't have seen if she hadn't stopped. A light that moved and bobbed and twirled slowly in the distance. Pulled away from the dance of the trees, the girl's attention was caught by the light, and she could not pull her eyes away from it. Then she heard the whisper of a voice. *'Remember.'* The sound, carried by the wind, whisked along her spine, up the back of her neck and into her ear. *'Remember.'* "

"Could it be a faery? she wondered. She'd heard about the faery folk, and it had been rumored that they did, indeed, inhabit portions of the dark woods. Could it be a leprechaun, carrying his pot of gold in one hand and his wee lantern in the other? Could it be a child, lost and afraid, in the midst of the dark woods with only a candle for light? Could it be the banshee searching for her next unsuspecting victim? A shiver ran down the girl's spine at the thought of the banshee flying from the dark woods toward the road and snatching her up in her skeletal arms."

"She started to walk away from the forest and once again heard the soft whisperings on the wind. *'Remember. Remember.'* The sound made her shiver, and she started to run, afraid of whatever it was in the woods. She heard the crunch, crunch sounds of her feet against the dead leaves on the road. She heard the soft panting sounds her own breath made as she ran as quickly as she could. She heard the wind whistling through the trees. She still heard the voice. *'Remember. Remember.'* And she saw that the light was coming closer to the road."

"She glanced around frantically. She could see a tiny light in the distance, and she knew it was the lantern that her father put on their barn to guide her safely home. All she had to do was make it to the barn, and she would be safe. She tried to run faster, but her legs were tired and her breathing labored. She knew that soon she would have to stop to catch her breath, or she would fall to the ground. But before she could slow down, she stumbled over a stone and tumbled to the ground."

"No sooner had she fallen than the light emerged from the woods. It was her worst nightmare come true. The terrible banshee, an ancient, glowing crone with fingers like the silvering tree branches, eyes like glowing coals, and teeth darkened with lichen and moss. The young girl covered her face with her hands. 'Will you remember me?' the banshee asked. The little girl nodded, her body shaking in fear. 'Will you remember me in a year?' the banshee demanded. The girl nodded again. 'Yes,' she whimpered. 'I will.' The banshee screamed into the night sky. 'Will you remember me in five years?' the old crone demanded. 'Yes,' the child pledged. The banshee moved closer, and the girl could feel its cold breath on her neck. 'Will you,' the crone asked slowly, 'always remember me?' With tears running down her cheeks, the girl nodded. 'Yes, always,' she said."

"The banshee didn't move, but stayed just hovering above the frightened child for what seemed to be an eternity. Finally, drawing a skeletal finger along the child's cheek, the creature spoke again. 'Knock, knock," it cackled. Confused, the child looked up. 'Who's there?' she whispered. The old crone's eyes widened, and her ember-like eyes glowed hotter than before. Her face contorted, and she lifted her claw-like hands up above the girl. 'What? You forgot me already?'"

It took a moment for the ending to register with Clarissa. Then her wide eyes crinkled, and she shook her head. "Grandpa, that wasn't a real story, was it?" she laughed.

Timothy held up his right hand. "On my honor," he said. "It happened to my great-great-grandaunt in the hills of Killarney when she was but a wee lass. Luckily she made it home to tell the tale."

"And ever since it happened," Sean said, standing up and walking across the room towards the refreshments, "knock-knock jokes were banned from the O'Reilly household."

Clarissa shook her head. "No," she said, looking to Mary for confirmation.

Mary laughed and shook her head. "I think they might be pulling your leg," she said. "But, my dear, now it's time for bed."

Bradley stood up. "Come on, Clarissa," he said. "Say goodnight, and then I'll help you get ready."

It took a few minutes, but finally Clarissa was climbing the stairs with Bradley, happily exchanging knock-knock jokes with him.

"Thank you, Da," Mary said. "That was the perfect story."

"The poor, sweet lass had eyes as wide as saucers before I started," he laughed. "And she should, after a night like this one. But I wanted to send her to bed with laughter on her lips, not a ghost under the bed."

"You are an excellent grandpa," Mary said, placing a kiss on his forehead.

"Well, and thank you for the ability to be a grandpa," he said, and then he looked around the room and scowled. "Since none of your brothers seem to be in any hurry to pass on the O'Reilly name."

"It's not our fault," Art said. "We look too much like you, so none of the girls will have us."

Margaret chuckled and pulled herself out of her chair. "Well, you bunch of ugly boys," she said, "come help me clean up. I'll not be leaving Mary with a mess like this."

"Oh, no, Ma, you've done too much," Mary said.

Margaret came over to her daughter and embraced her. "It's not often that I can be helpful, and tonight I'm going to insist. You need to rest after what you've been through today," she said. "If not for you, then for the baby. You go to bed, Mary O'Reilly Alden before I have your father carry you up."

"But, Ma," Mary argued.

Margaret placed her hands on her hips and shook her head. "To bed with you," she said. "Now.

We'll all be here in the morning, so we can catch up then."

"Goodnight, Mary," her brothers called mockingly. "Sleep tight."

She chuckled. "Goodnight," she replied.

Chapter Fifty-nine

Moonlight flooded in through the bedroom window, illuminating the entire room as Mary padded back from the bathroom for the third time that night. She sighed. When would she remember to stop drinking liquids after nine o'clock?

She was nearly to the bed when the closet door started to slowly open. Clutching the bed post, she watched in silent awe as the door swung open even further. "Um, we have a rule now," she whispered. "No more bedroom visits. The bedroom and the bathroom are off limits."

The moving door stopped.

"See, I told you," a voice whispered. "It was right on the instructions."

"Instructions? What instructions?" another voice replied. "We're dead. Who needs instructions?"

"Well, obviously you do," the first voice said. "Just like you always needed directions but never asked."

"We got to where we were going, didn't we?" the second voice replied.

"I don't think death was our destination," the first voice said.

"Oh, and now you're going to blame me for that?" the second voice asked.

"Shut the door, Frasier. We don't want to disturb her," the first voice ordered.

"Oh, sure, don't disturb her," Frasier replied. "Don't think about…"

The door closed, shutting off their conversation.

Mary stared at the door for a moment and then started to laugh.

Tomorrow is certainly going to be another interesting day.

The End

About the author: Terri Reid lives near Freeport, the home of the Mary O'Reilly Mystery Series, and loves a good ghost story. She lives in a hundred year-old farmhouse complete with its own ghost. She loves hearing from her readers at author@terrireid.com

Other Books by Terri Reid:

Mary O'Reilly Paranormal Mystery Series:

Loose Ends (Book One)

Good Tidings (Book Two)

Never Forgotten (Book Three)

Final Call (Book Four)

Darkness Exposed (Book Five)

Natural Reaction (Book Six)

Secret Hollows (Book Seven)

Broken Promises (Book Eight)

Twisted Paths (Book Nine)

Veiled Passages (Book Ten)

Bumpy Roads (Book Eleven)

Treasured Legacies (Book Twelve)

Buried Innocence (Book Thirteen)

Stolen Dreams (Book Fourteen)

Haunted Tales (Book Fifteen)

Mary O'Reilly Short Stories

Irish Mists – Sean's Story

The Three Wise Guides

Tales Around the Jack O'Lantern

PRCD Case Files:

The Ghosts Of New Orleans -A Paranormal Research and Containment Division Case File

Eochaidh:

Legend of the Horseman (Book One)

Romance:

Bearly in Love

The Order of Brigid's Cross:

 The Order of Brigid's Cross – The Wild Hunt (Book One)

If you enjoy the Mary O'Reilly Paranormal Mystery Series – you might enjoy these books:

Five-stars for the Wild Hunt!

The child's story is too far-fetched for most of the Chicago Police Force to believe – claims of an army of other-worldly creatures who attacked and dismembered the rival gangs. But Sean O'Reilly believes him, because he's seen them himself. An encounter he had as a boy in a dark forest in Ireland did not just give him nightmares, but changed his entire life.

Terri hit this one out of the park with a home run! I love Sean and all the other characters that she brought to life in these pages as well as a few old friends that lend their support!! Great Job Terri Reid!

"Full of thrills and chills, a fun rollercoaster ride of a book!"
~Susan Andersen, New York Times Bestselling author

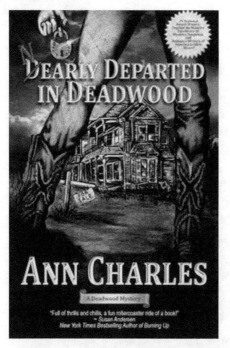

NEARLY DEPARTED IN DEADWOOD, the first book in the on-going Deadwood Mystery Series, a Top-Rated #1 Kindle Bestseller in BOTH Women Sleuth and Ghost genres!

WINNER of the 2010 Daphne du Maurier Award for Excellence in Mystery/Suspense

WINNER of the 2011 Romance Writers of America® Golden Heart Award for Best Novel with Strong Romantic Elements

HAUNTED
A Bridgeton Park Cemetery Book

Not everyone is haunted, but everyone has a ghost story.

"...Something was coming from her mother's end of the hall, he thought. Could he really perceive a shadow that was darker than the dark itself? Or were his eyes playing tricks? Whatever the case, he could feel something coming towards him. There was a vast coldness approaching Cassie's bedroom, a wall of ice bearing down on him inexorably, eating up the distance between them until he felt the first of its wintry presence against his face..."

CPSIA information can be obtained
at www.ICGtesting.com
Printed in the USA
LVHW080810011118
595590LV00021B/300/P

9 781514 252581